OUTPOST INFINITY

By
RAYMOND F. JONES

I0616904

ARMCHAIR FICTION
PO Box 4369, Medford, Oregon 97504

*For more information about Armchair Books and products, visit our
website at…*

www.armchairfiction.com

Or email us at…

armchairfiction@yahoo.com

A VOYAGE INTO THE
MORASS OF INFINITY

The Tantalus Express was a top-of-the-line passenger ship, carrying her travelers incredible distances amounting to thousands of light years. But tonight she was overdue—late by a meager six minutes. Yet those back on Earth knew that even being a few seconds late spelled disaster for the 2500 passengers and crew. They knew the Express was lost somewhere in an unknown realm that even the most brilliant scientists could only conceive of in abstract theoretical terms. And now, adrift in the terrible grayness beyond the universe, the passengers and crew of the Express waited hopelessly for death…while Carl Mayhew, the only man who could aid them, plunged ever deeper into the multiplying coils of outer darkness—where every road leads away from safe, normal Earth, toward—Outpost Infinity!

FOR A SECOND COMPLETE NOVEL, TURN TO PAGE 85

CAST OF CHARACTERS

CARL MAYHEW
He was the chief engineer for Trans-Astra—and he was brilliant; but some aspects of infinity were still mind-bending even for him.

SUSAN DAWNING
This movie star had a reputation for wild tabloid romances, but underneath it all was a woman with grit and a heart of gold.

CAPTAIN DRANGUE
He commanded a space liner that made its voyages in a fraction of a second; to take any longer might spell doom for all aboard.

WARREN
As ship's psychiatrist, he knew that 2500 passengers lost in an unknown plane of infinity were bound to get a little edgy.

CALVERT MASON
He was one of the greatest semanticists of all time, and he would soon give new meaning to the expression: "Double Homicide."

JEFFREY WICKS
Emotionally unstable and a complete drunken lout at times—but was he a threat to the safety of those around him?

JACK SEBASTIAN
He was on duty the night the Tantalus Express turned up missing; and he knew immediately it was gone—simply gone.

CHAPTER ONE
Beyond the Alephs

THE FLOOD of light within the Central Operations room of Trans-Astra fought back the night that pressed against the windows. To Sebastian it seemed as if all the black terror of the infinities were washing down, tearing at the Terminal to uproot that symbol of man's daring.

He shook himself and moved away from the black squares of the windows overlooking the darkened city. Inside, the blaze of light was warm and comforting. And now the communications panel was brightening in response to his call to Tantalus. Peters, the Tantalus operator, appeared on the screen.

"Where's the *Express*?" Jack demanded. "Can't it ever leave on time? Did you let some dame who'd forgotten her poodle hold up the whole ship?"

Peters' face whitened, and for a moment he was unable to speak. "The *Express* left six minutes ago. Hasn't it—?"

The Operations Room seemed suddenly still. So this was it, Sebastian thought.

He glanced out again towards the ominous blackness of night that hovered over the Terminal. On the opposite side of the building he could see the vast landing area—still empty.

Compensation, he thought. *You can't forever send ships out into the utter unknown and always fish them back. There'll be losses until you know just where those ships are going.* Of course, Mayhew and the other high-powered physicists called such fears ignorant superstition. Sebastian was well grounded in theory, and only Carl Mayhew was a better technician than he was, but he had always been haunted by the fear that they would some day be unable to pull back a ship they had sent into the black, unknown hole of the transfinities.

Now it had happened and the *Tantalus Express*, with twenty-five hundred passengers and crewmen, was gone— simply gone.

Peters was saying, "Seventeen thousand light years is a long way. Maybe they'll show up. Six minutes isn't very long."

"Six seconds would have been too long, and you know it," snapped Jack savagely. "Check time coordinates with me." Peters secured a section of his recorder chart showing the complex time-coordinate curves prior to and following the departure of the ship for Earth. As Jack read off his ordinates recorded on Earth, Peters called off the corresponding abscissa points on Tantalus.

"They check, said Jack resignedly. He had known they would. He knew also that there was no hurry to make the next move. There was absolutely no way of ever locating the ship and the twenty-five hundred men and women it carried.

But Mayhew would want to make an attempt at searching for the ship in the Raft as soon as possible. Jack ordered the Tantalus operator crisply, "Stay on call. We may want you later. That's all for now."

The screen darkened in the midst of the distant operator's protests. Why should he have to stay up the rest of the night? There was nothing he could do...

Immediately, Sebastian put in a call to Mayhew's apartment. The chief engineer's face appeared almost instantly, as if he had been waiting for the call, but his eyes were still puffy with sleep.

"What is it?" he snapped. "Do you need me there?"

"The *Tantalus Express*—" said Sebastian. "Gone. We need you as fast as you can get here."

Mayhew's eyes cleared; and that was the only sign he gave. "Right." He cut off.

Sebastian felt better already. The responsibility was passing from his shoulders to those of the one man most capable of accepting it. And that load had weighed heavily on him.

Men sensitive enough to understand the full significance and responsibility of what they were doing could not long bear up under the strain of Trans-Astra work. That was why the early operators had been replaced by less sensitive men, to whom the throwing of a switch to send the great *Express* into the unknown was like running a streetcar.

But there had to be sensitive men in key spots, men who understood as nearly as possible the exact limits of what they were doing. Jack Sebastian was one of these. The operator on Tantalus who could throw a switch or repair an atomic motor, but who had absolutely no understanding of the transfinite, was the other kind. He could not see any reason why a ship on a seventeen-thousand-light-year journey should not take six minutes or sixty minutes instead of arriving instantaneously. And that was all to the good, for if he had possessed Sebastian's full capacity to grasp the situation, he probably would have blown his brains out for what he had done when he'd sent the *Express* into the transfinite—from which it was not going to return.

MAYHEW arrived at the Terminal in so short a time that it scarcely seemed possible he'd had time to dress. As unperturbed as if he were there only to replace a broken tube, he hung his coat in a locker and began to examine the records and meters that told the story of the functioning of the receiving equipment.

"I'm afraid you're becoming careless, Jack," said Mayhew as he bent over the records on a desk.

"What's the matter?" Sebastian's heart pounded.

"The guide beam. We've definitely established that a thirty-minute warm-up period is absolutely necessary for stability. Yet I see that you had the beam on only nineteen minutes before the *Express* took off."

"I won't say that it's not my fault," said Jack. "But that crazy dope on Tantalus was apparently asleep. I couldn't connect with him until nineteen minutes before takeoff, and—well, the charts seemed to indicate stability, so I didn't order him to hold the ship. Do you think that was responsible?"

Mayhew shook his head. "No," the chief engineer said. "It wasn't lack of stability of the guide beam, but this is an exhibition of carelessness. Where it occurs once it might occur again, or might have already occurred in some other detail. How would you like to transfer to the lab for a few weeks' rest?"

Sebastian sighed resignedly. "The bone heap, huh? I guess that's it if you say so. Anyway, my bimonthly check is coming up next week. I guess the squirrel docs would have thrown me out anyway."

It wouldn't be so bad, Sebastian thought. The lab was a nice place to work and you didn't feel like a potential mass executioner every time you threw a switch. He'd never understand a man like Mayhew. Mayhew ran the whole show; the strain should have been greater on him than on anyone else. Yet he never showed any sign of it; he was always the same—irritable, but supremely sane.

Mayhew plowed further into the maze of operational reports. Sebastian left him as a newcomer entered the room on the far side, away from the equipment. He was talking to Bailey and Michels, two of the minor technicians, as Sebastian came up. The newcomer was Harris, from the ticket office downstairs.

"What can we tell these people?" Harris asked. "They're getting impatient and worried. I'm afraid there's going to be trouble if we don't explain the delay."

Sebastian went to the window and looked over the ramp and waiting area before the huge enclosure where the *Express* should have been. Here were the usual crowds of newsmen, photographers, relatives, lovers, and friends who greeted the passengers of every ship. But there was no ship bearing those they expected to greet—and there never would be. In each of those lives out there, and less remotely, in thousands of others, a tragic blankness would forever exist because of the failure of the transfinite process to function one single time.

He realized suddenly that it was tragic not only because of that loss, but because it meant the end of Trans-Astra. His mind recoiled. A moment before he had felt regret over transfer to the lab. Why, in a week there would be no lab, no Trans-Astra! The public would never permit it to go on after this disaster.

He turned back to Harris. "I could tell you what to tell the crowd," he said, "but you'd probably better not tell it to them now. See Mayhew. It's his show now. Eventually the world will have to know the ship is never coming in, but perhaps not now."

Harris turned away and walked over to Mayhew. Sebastian wondered how far civilization among the far planets of the universe would be set back by the events of this night. Going back to the slow atomic-powered ships would expand the universe and shrink man's conquests to an infinitesimal fraction of what they might have been—if the transfinite had not failed.

MAYHEW showed his first sign of irritation as Harris came up. "What is it, Harris? Surely your department is enough to manage, or would you like to run this end, too?"

"I'm sorry, Mr. Mayhew, but that crowd out there is becoming, well—very ugly. I'm afraid there'll be serious consequences if we don't tell them something definite soon. I thought perhaps you could suggest—"

"Tell them the *Express* was held up on Tantalus. Does it take brains to think of a simple thing like that?"

"It's too late, Mr. Mayhew. We've already told them the ship departed on time. And they know that arrival is instantaneous. That's why they're becoming ugly. They're afraid. They're beginning to generate rumors—"

Rumors, Mayhew thought. Yes, there would be rumors; they dated back to the earliest days of transfinite experiments—ghastly rumors of horrors lurking in the *interim* just beyond the veil of reality, ready to lunge out upon an unsuspecting humanity if man were fool enough to rend that veil. He had fought those rumors long ago and knew he would have to fight them the rest of his life, until the nature of the *interim* was established in terms of physical experience.

"Tell them," he said to Harris, "that power troubles developed in the *interim,* that we are in communication with the *Express* and all aboard are well. Tell them I am leaving to enter the *interim* and supervise the repair work necessary to allow the ship to continue. Tell them to go home—that public announcement of the arrival will be made when it is possible to do so."

Harris stared in unbelief. "But you don't mean that, Mr. Mayhew. The *interim*—Rodney and Welcher—"

"—were particularly unfortunate. But we know a lot more than we did in their day. Now get out!"

Harris whirled away from the mounting irritation of the chief engineer, but halted at Mayhew's commanding "Harris!"

"Yes, sir."

"Who's aboard the *Express?* Anybody?"

"Everybody. That's what makes it so difficult. It's the usual weekend crowd. Governor Wesson of the Southern Sector. Susan Dawning, the actress; Jeffry Wicks and his uncle. Calvert Mason. James Darrell, the author—"

"Okay." Mayhew waved him away. He turned to Sebastian. "Who was master this trip?"

Jack glanced at the records on his own desk. "Drangue was handling the ship. He's as good a man as we've got."

Mayhew grunted in disgust. "A streetcar conductor! But that's the kind of men we have to pick to keep them from going crazy after a couple of trips. All right, I've got all the information I can get here. The *Express* is out there in the *interim* somewhere, but in which Aleph is going to be a problem to determine."

"But you aren't going into the *interim* and—stop!" Sebastian exploded. "That would be suicide. Rodney and Welcher proved you can't wander around in the *interim* at will."

"Why do you think I've been working on the Raft for the past three years? You'll note that exactly two days after it is finished I have the first opportunity to test it in actual search for a lost ship. There's a neat problem in causation, and it can be handled by straightforward math it you can find a point to get hold of it. Try your hand at it while I'm gone."

SEBASTIAN walked silently beside Mayhew as the latter went to the other end of the Operations room. There, massive panels of intricate equipment loomed almost as bulky as the main transmitters and receivers of the Terminal.

This mass of electronic equipment was the Raft and its associated transmitter and receiver. The Raft proper was simply a huge mesh cage, a cube about twelve feet on a side. It was crammed with panel-mounted tubes, transformers, recorders, switches and a score of nameless pieces of equipment that had evolved from Mayhew's brain.

Above the Raft was a copper plate eight inches thick, and below it in the floor was a similar plate. Great cables snaked from these plates to the inwards of the massed panels surrounding the Raft.

"You're sure it will work?" said Sebastian dubiously.

"I know it. You watch for my call. We're being controlled by factors of causation that will make it impossible to fail—I hope," He grinned wryly.

Jack knew what he meant. Causation was still an infant science, but the implications already uncovered by it were staggering. There were indications that certain main lines of human endeavor were inevitably destined to succeed, and any effort that could be aligned to aid one of the successful event streams would be ultimately successful—though not always in the manner desired. There was some evidence that the implacable religious faith of some of the ancient saints was simply an intuitive half understanding of the principles of causation. Mayhew firmly believed that the development of the science of the transfinite was just such a major success stream as causation indicated. Sebastian wondered if it were this firm conviction—this almost religious faith—that enabled him to bear the psychological burden of his position so successfully.

Mayhew passed between the panels and opened the door of the mesh cage. He settled himself in the control chair before the myriad meters and switches that controlled the functioning of the Raft. At last he signaled Sebastian with a wave of his hand. Sebastian switched on the transmitter, and from the depths of the equipment came the sounds of snapping relays and heavy plungers being driven home. Finally, the massive poles of the switch energizing the great copper plates crashed into their sockets.

Instantly, a white aura engulfed the Raft. Through it Mayhew waved reassuringly to Sebastian, then reached forward and threw a switch. In that instant, the Raft disappeared, leaving only the slowly dying aura to show that anything had rested between those burnished copper plates.

For a long time Jack Sebastian stood staring at the empty space. He had no way of knowing then that he would never see Carl Mayhew again, but as he looked out—towards the vacant landing area of the Terminal—he was certain of it. That emptiness between the copper plates was like a doorway into hell, that gateway to all the infinities of creation. And when he looked out into the cold darkness that bore unyieldingly upon the Terminal, he sensed that Trans-Astra had sent its last ship across the *interim*. The slow, clumsy, atomic-powered ships were already hissing through space in the background of his mind. They'd come back, because Carl Mayhew and the *Tantalus Express* never would.

CHAPTER TWO
The Wheel of Infinity

THE TRANSFINITE!

From almost the moment that ancient man learned to count, his mind leaped ahead in vain, metaphysical struggling to grasp the final number beyond which there were no numbers.

Infinity.

It was the ancient mathematician, Georg Cantor, who, in the nineteenth century, defined infinity and assigned a symbol to the number beyond all numbers.

Cantor appropriated the first letter, Aleph, of the Hebrew alphabet to define the cardinality of the ordinals in an infinite series. Aleph-Null became the first of the multitude of infinite classes, whose discovery was the foundation stone of a new and incredible universe.

Infinity.

Consider a number n. Now, n may be reached by a process of mathematical induction beginning with zero. That is,

0, 1, 2, 3, 4, 5,...n.

But not Aleph-Null, or N_0. It is the number of all the ordinals, and so cannot be reached by a process of mathematical induction. For:

N_0 plus 1 equals N_0.

N_0 plus or minus n equals N_0 (where n is any inductive number).

Likewise:

N_0^2 equals N_0; and: n times N_0 equals N_0.

This somewhat astonishing arithmetic of the infinite was demonstrated by Cantor, but an even more incredible property was shown when be proved that among infinite classes a part is as great as the whole, and the whole is no greater than some of its parts.

Consider the class of integers. The obvious assumption is that there are many more integers, even and odd, than there are odd integers. But let the set of odd integers be counted by placing them in one-to-one correspondence with the set of integers:

1 2 3 4 5 6 ...
1 3 5 7 9 11 ...

It is obvious that under every integer, even or odd, it is possible to place an odd integer, and the process may be continued without end!

The set of integers is infinite, but, since it is possible to establish a one-to-one correspondence between the set of integers and a part of the set of integers, the two sets have the same number of elements, *the same cardinality*. This cardinality of both sets is Aleph-Null. There are as many odd integers as there are integers. The part is as great as the whole.*

Besides, N_0, Cantor showed the existence of an entire series of Alephs, N_1, N_2, and N_3... in an infinite series. It was

---

*One of Cantor's greatest triumphs, however, came in proving that in spite of the unique arithmetic of N_0, there were classes whose cardinality did exceed N_0. The class of real numbers he proved to have a cardinality exceeding N_0.

The real numbers composed of the rational and irrational numbers includes the irrationals, which are not algebraic as well as those that are. The former are the transcendental numbers, Pi and e being the best-known examples, and almost the only known examples before Cantor's time.

It was known that the rational and algebraic numbers were denumerable, so Cantor had to prove that the class of transcendentals, of which only a handful were known, was too big to be counted by integers, that it had a cardinality exceeding N_0.

To his great credit, he succeeded in this, and the class of real numbers was found to have 2^{N_0} elements, which was easily shown to be greater than N_0.

never discovered, however, whether 2^{N_0} was one of the Alephs or not, but it was a very important concept to Trans-Astra, for it was the number of terms in a "continuous series" as Cantor defined it, and so was also the number of points in any measure of space, finite or infinite, or the number of instants of any measure of time.

An important corollary was that any finite measure of space or time has the same number of points or instants as any other finite or infinite measure of space or time.

With a sort of mathematical aloofness, then, the Alephs ignored the ordinary processes of addition and subtraction, multiplication and involution. But in the special case of $N_0^{N_0}$ an entirely new concept was created.

This new and greater number was designated by Cantor as C He never determined whether or not C was one of the Alephs, but he conceived the existence of higher and higher transfinite numbers created by repeated processes of involution, as C°, etc.

Mayhew, very early in his career, established a proof that C was not one of the Alephs, and this led directly to the processes by which Trans-Astra operated.

It had always been assumed that there were infinite collections, and various ways of "proving" this were brought forth. But even long after Cantor, mathematicians feared that all such proofs were fallacious.

It was Mayhew who finally proved the real existence of infinite collects, yet this reality was as difficult for the layman to comprehend as was the curved space of Einstein.

Mayhew proved that the universe of man belonged to such an infinite collection, that Aleph-Null was the cardinal number of this collection. But this proof did not mean that a man could get in a spaceship and travel to another identical Earth somewhere if he went far enough. The members of this Aleph-Null collection to which man's universe belonged existed congruently and co-temporally in space, its properties being such that Aleph-Null appears in all calculations and subjective and objective observations as unity.   For that reason, man was never aware of the multiple universe about him. It was impossible for him to observe it.

Impossible, until Mayhew.

Mayhew demonstrated the nature of C, and the existence of sets having this cardinal number.   He did the original experimental work of electrical field transformation that made it possible for a member of an Aleph-Null set to transfer to a C set. Having gone that far, it was impossible to return to the Aleph-Null set, but at a different point than the point of origin.   Thus began the revolution in interstellar transportation.

Within two years, Trans-Astra had wiped out the five-hundred-billion-dollar space transport system based on the slow atomic-powered vessels, which had difficulty in attaining a velocity of even a quarter c.

But utilization of the transfinite was not without its drawbacks. The first experimenters who had personally gone into a C set or the *interim,* as it came to be known in transport jargon, were subjected to stimuli that no human senses could endure. There were no names for those stimuli. They had no parallels in human observational history. The men came back mad.   They were Rodney and Welcher, and their fate remained a horror to deter all who would dare the *interim.*

It was determined that their difficulty had been due to stopping in the *interim* and also lack of proper electrical field protection to shield them from the unwanted stimuli. Actual transport of ships was now accomplished with a timeless interval within the *interim.* This prevented any results of the kind Rodney and Welcher experienced, as did also the heavy electrical fields protecting the ship.   But the public still remembered Rodney and Welcher.

It had long been Mayhew's dream to explore the *interim,* and to this end he had designed the Raft, which bore heavy fields to protect the occupant. It was self-propulsive, once it left the set of Aleph-Null, and therefore made independent exploration of the *interim* possible.

Mayhew had also in the back of his mind that it would serve as an excellent lifeboat should a ship ever be lost. But that had never occurred since the beginning of Trans-Astra…until now.

AUTOMATIC controls were set to halt the Raft in the realm of C. To Carl Mayhew, transfer was instantaneous. It seemed like the sudden thrusting of a gray, translucent blanket over the Raft and the simultaneous removal of gravity. Nausea oozed through him and his senses rebelled against the blind, gray world that surrounded him.

He had no explanation for the phenomena of his environment, but he suspected that much of it was due to his protective fields and that it would have appeared quite different without them. He turned to concentrate on the instrument panel before him.

The method by which he hoped to locate the *Express* was simple in principle. The *Express* was lost somewhere in the Infinities of space-times composing the C system. By sending a probing guide beam into each of these N_0 systems he would eventually obtain a response when his beam coincided with the beam constantly being emitted by the *Tantalus Express.* The *Express* beam could not possibly be inactive; it was a radiation induced in the metal of the ship's structure and would outlast the ship itself.

Since in any finite measure of time there were a greater number of instants than there were time systems in the entire C set, it became simply a problem of counting the N_0 number of time systems and identifying the one containing the missing ship.

He had the instruments to accomplish this. They formed an integral part of the Raft. By selecting a given measure of time—one minute, for example—he could place every one of the N_0 time systems into one-to-one correspondence with an instant of time within that minute. By so counting, he could determine the time system in which the *Express* lay.

Mayhew pressed the controls to begin the counting process. He was bothered less by the gray fog now…except when he thought of what it might be like out there without the protection of the Raft. It was not a healthy speculation.

Abruptly, Mayhew jerked his head towards the chronometer on the panel. Two and a half minutes had elapsed. The counting process had passed through that many cycles.

Not a sign of response had come from the indicator.

Mayhew frowned. Closely, he watched while another cycle passed. He checked the meters. The equipment seemed in order. He switched off momentarily and then tried once again, never taking his eyes away from the meter that would indicate coincidence.

But that minute passed without response. He changed the counting cycle to occupy ten minutes, though he knew that was ridiculous from the standpoint of transfinite principles. One second would have been as adequate as an hour.

There was nothing at all.

Nothing but that gray fog and the rising, wavelike motion of the Raft that sent torrents of nausea through him. Failure stripped away his protective cloak of confidence.

This had been his only card to play, his ace in the hole, and he had banked on it with the confidence that the laws of causation were on his side, because he was in a success stream of endeavor. The implications of failure overwhelmed him. It meant that exploitation of the transfinite was not a success stream after all.

He did not know how long it might have been that he simply sat there staring at the panel with its dead indicator as the spatial counting cycle surged from one to Aleph-Null and back again, scores of times. His mind dropped its mathematical sophistication, and he thought in the terms his technicians used—lost in infinity. He was thinking of the twenty-five hundred persons aboard the *Tantalus Express*. They were as nonexistent as if they had never been born.

It began to ring through his brain—*lost in infinity—lost in infinity—lost—*

Then the fun significance of that mathematically non-semantic term hit him.

Infinity.

That included the topmost limit of the limitless hierarchy of the Alephs. And he had been exploring only the infinitesimal fragment represented by C.

Normal operation of the Trans-Astra ships did not extend beyond C. But the only possible explanation for the facts before Mayhew was that the *Express* had somehow jumped beyond C into C^o or to an even higher set. If that were true, the number of operations necessary to test for the presence of the ship would itself be an infinite set, possibly of the magnitude of C itself. A hopeless task.

But—it was just conceivable that the *Express* had gone no farther than C^o. He considered the problem of manipulating the Raft into that set. It had never been designed for such an operation, but he turned to the calculator built into the control desk and began pounding the keys in a bewildering stream of transfinite computations.

After an hour he was convinced that the Raft could be driven at least into C^o and possibly one higher set. It was a start, anyway.

The changes in the circuits of the Raft involved only precise re-evaluations of the forces applied. Taking these values from his computations, Mayhew set them into the circuits. Then, without hesitation, he threw the controls that put the Raft into a cross-stream through the infinities.

THE SWIRLING gray universe congealed about the Raft as if it were a bug caught in amber. An hysterical claustrophobia seized Mayhew so suddenly that it was inside his mental defenses before he recognized the symptoms. His hands shook and he stood up to beat against that implacable prison wall of gray that extended to the infinite bounds of space. He felt that it would be horrible to die, as he was going to die, in this unknown prison beyond all normal human experience.

Then, just as suddenly as they had formed, the gray walls began to melt. Their substance flowed away like dirty ice melting in the rays of a spring sun. Mayhew collapsed in the seat and leaned his head on the desk of the control board.

He was weak and trembling from the hysteric seizure. He had never thought himself susceptible to such complete loss of mental control. The knowledge that any force could so overcome him was in itself shattering.

He began to understand what might have happened to Rodney and Welcher.

Like a clearing storm, the grayness vanished. His indicators showed that he himself was somewhere within a C° set, probably the first human being knowingly to enter the set.

He seemed to be in an illusory state of motion. He was in the center of a vast, shining green plain. In the distance, walls of flowing light rose abruptly and continued beyond his range of vision. The plain seemed to encompass the sum of all the infinite space through which he had passed. Yet the walls of flowing, spinning light that bounded it were within range of finite senses. Or were they? Perhaps his senses were now infinite, partaking of the characteristics of the set in which he was located. That aspect of the problem, the physiological effect, was one that the transfinite equations ignored.

But now the nausea, the fear, and the terror of the C set were gone. Mayhew relaxed his grip on the panel and stood up. If the *Express* were lost here, perhaps those aboard didn't want to come back, he thought.

It was an idyllic lotus land. The peacefulness of that endless plain and the flowing light-falls washed away all care and all uneasiness. Yet in the very peacefulness and contentment of it there was a certain hideous aspect that was alien to human senses. It was as if all activity, all desire, had suddenly ended here in complete satiation and that it mattered not at all if he ever found the *Tantalus Express* or not.

He fought down the suggestion that crept into the cells of his brain, and increased the strength of the field about the Raft. He wondered if it were not entirely possible that those aboard the *Express* had been overcome by this stimulus.

He switched on the counter circuits, which he had revised to count the C sets as they had counted the Aleph sets previously.

As the circuit warmed up, the indicator needle suddenly swung over. Mayhew grunted with satisfaction. He was on the trail of the missing *Express* at last.

But his satisfaction died as he scowled at the meter. It had suddenly dropped back to a negative position, as if the *Express* had slipped out of the C set it had been in. The circuit returned to null and started the counting process again. Abruptly, there was a positive indication—but it was not in the same C set as previously. Then the contact was lost once more.

Sweat broke out on Mayhew's brow. The *Express* was moving transversely across the sets composing C°. This was the insoluble problem. Two objects searching for each other, both moving, would never meet in any finite period.

Then he considered the problem more closely. If the *Express* passed through his own set just once, he could set off the arrival alarm within the ship by means of the guide beam. But how to make the *Express* pass through his set? He could send the Raft through the entire infinity of sets and the alarm would go off all right, but Drangue would still not be able to get to Mayhew's set because it would be changing.

He put a recorder on the counter and observed the blips that indicated the ship's presence. After a moment he took renewed hope. Drangue was following a definite sequence, apparently spiraling through the sets of C° hoping to hit his home Aleph. What he didn't know was that he was in C° instead of C

When he was sure that he had the sequence plotted correctly, Mayhew set up the calculator to predict the future path of the *Express*. After ten minutes' work he had this determined. He moved the Raft onto a point on the trajectory and waited. Recorder pens now indicated his own position and the path of the *Express*.

For a seeming eternity he waited while the pens traced the collision course. And suddenly the lines crossed. Mayhew looked about, straining his senses for some manifestation of the *Express*. For an instant the counter needle pounded the pin madly, then abruptly dropped back to null setting.

They had missed. The alarm must not have gone off in the *Express*; or else Drangue was not in control and the ship was wandering helplessly.

He was about to shift the Raft to a new position ahead of the *Express*, but suddenly the line showing the path of the ship turned and slowly traced its way back to the line of the Raft's position.

Mayhew leaped expectantly towards his communication plate. The instant the lines touched he spoke into the microphone. "Mayhew calling Flight Thirty-one, *Tantalus Express*. Calling Flight Thirty-one."

The harried face of Drangue came into view on the screen for an instant, then faded. His lips moved as if in startled exclamation, but his image vanished before any word could be tittered.

Mayhew's fingers sought the controls of the Raft. Swiftly, he jockeyed the machine down the infinities, watching the lines upon the recorder. Once again the face of Drangue appeared, and Mayhew exclaimed, "Stop! Hold it!"

The image wavered, then solidified and held.

CHAPTER THREE
Tweedledum and Tweedledee

"MAYHEW!" Drangue exclaimed. "What's happened? Where are we?"

"Hold your position," Mayhew ordered. "I'll come aboard."

He looked out over the plains of light, wondering if the ship was in range of his vision or if he'd have to hunt through space for it.

He didn't. There in the distance it lay, like an angular blob against the distant shimmering falls of light. Though it was visible due to the characteristics of this realm of C°, Mayhew suspected that the *Express* might be light years from him. He was certain that this peaceful plain before him constituted the entire range of C°.

The Raft began to move slowly under its own power towards the distant ship. Mayhew's theory was soon confirmed. The *Express* was an inestimable distance from him. It grew no larger at all in his sight. He stepped up the velocity, utilizing all the power of the atomic engines in the Raft, until he gained a velocity of eight tenths of a light year per second. Only after minutes at this velocity did the *Express* begin to grow appreciably larger. Mayhew thought he had set some kind of a record for naked-eye vision. Oculists, at least, would find no business in the world of C°.

The *Tantalus Express* looked nothing like a ship in the accepted sense of the word, any more than the Raft did. Rather, it looked like a moderately sized, four-story building with rectangular floor area. Its facades of glass were lavishly ablaze with light, just as they must have been at the moment of takeoff.

As he approached, Mayhew could see the passengers gaping at the incredible world of C° and his own tiny Raft—which must have seemed like some alien monster bearing down upon them.

He drew up at last to the main port of the ship and let the protective field of the Raft coalesce with that of the *Express*. It was, of course, impossible for human life to exist outside the protection of the ships. Mayhew wondered if it were cold or hot, airless or otherwise out there. But that was something man might never know. Instruments could not operate through the protective fields and without a means of correlation any independent data taken out there would be meaningless. But that was all another problem.

The port of the *Express* opened and Captain Drangue rushed out, a portly little man with a florid face and no imagination.

"Man, are we glad to see you!" he exclaimed. "We thought we were goners for sure when we just faded off into this stuff and didn't make the landing terminal. What the devil happened, anyway?"

"That's what I want you to tell me," said Mayhew. "Apparently something slipped and sent you into C° instead of merely transferring you into C and back again."

Drangue's face grew pale. "C°! No one's ever been there before. Why it—"

"—isn't half as bad as it might be, is it?" Mayhew smiled. "It's just the crazy rumors about the transfinite that make people think there should be seven-legged dragons breathing fire out here. In fact, it's rather pleasant and peaceful. I thought at first that maybe you had all decided to stay here because it was nicer than Earth."

Drangue shuddered. "Not me. This business is just too weird for my taste. The sooner we get back to Earth, the better."

As they entered the promenade deck, they caught sight of a group of passengers. One of the men in the group was talking excitedly to the others and the confused state of mind of all them was evident.

"I'm sure glad you've come," said Drangue. "These people are terrified. Warren, the ship psychiatrist, says their emotional tension is approaching the danger point. Maybe your presence will drop it a notch or two."

Just then several of the group turned and recognized Mayhew. An excited, bald-headed man jumped in his path.

"Mr. Mayhew!" he exclaimed. "You'll never know how thankful we are to see you. Do you think you can get us out of this terrible predicament?"

"Probably in time for breakfast on Earth."

"How can you speak of food under these circumstances?" a middle-aged matron, obviously suffering from nervous stomach, spoke up. "I shan't touch a bite until this tragic business is over!"

A young man, obviously very drunk, staggered forward. "The great Mayhew!" he said. "Got's trapped out here an' now you think you can keep's happy with a big, fat, noble gesture! Nuts! Whyn't you tell's we're all as good as dead?"

Mayhew turned to Drangue. "Is this one of the local natives or did you bring him along?"

"That's Jeffry Wicks," said Drangue sourly. "I've had to threaten to throw him in the brig twice already. Once he gets drunk it seems to be permanent. His uncle promised to—"

"I'm sorry, Captain Drangue." A gray-haired man came after young Wicks. "I left the door of the room open when I hurried out in the excitement of hearing that a rescue party was on the way. I'll be more careful until Jeff sobers up."

Though Mayhew had never met him before, he knew something of Calvert Mason. The man was one of the greatest semanticists of all time. But apparently even that didn't help him in rearing his nephew.

"Leggo me!" Wicks demanded as his uncle grasped his arm. "Cut me outa y'r will—an' what good d'you think all y'r lousy money's gonna do now? Mayhew's got's trapped an' we'll all be dead soon."

"It's all right. Mr. Mason," said Drangue. "We're about out of the woods now, I think. Have you met Mr. Mayhew? He's our chief engineer, and the man who gets the rest of us out of trouble with this transfinite business."

"How do you do?" said Mason. "Will it be long, now?"

Mayhew nodded greetings and found himself liking the stolid, gray-haired Mason.

"It won't be long, Mr. Mason. I'm sure of it," he said.

AS MASON and Wicks broke through the crowd to get back to their rooms, a young woman placed a hand on Mayhew's arm. He recognized her instantly as Susan Dawning, singer and actress of the airscreens.

"I'm Susan Dawning," she said. "I want you to know that you can count on me for any help I can give." Her smile was something Mayhew thought he would remember all his life.

But he knew Miss Dawning—by reputation—as did practically every other citizen on Earth. Her current romances, a new one almost every couple of months, made headlines constantly. Mayhew had always thought of her as a very neurotic, unstable young woman, a type he disliked.

"Thank you," he said rather shortly. "But I'm sure we'll get along all right."

"Don't fool yourself," said Drangue. "Miss Dawning has been one of the company's most valuable assets since we became lost. She's kept up the morale of the passengers wonderfully. Warren says they might have gone over the danger line if it hadn't been for Miss Dawning. We'll owe her a great deal of thanks when this is over.

"I'm sure we will," said Mayhew. And Miss Dawning would have a considerable amount of new, free publicity, he thought.

With Drangue, he finally broke away from the crowd and made his way to the control room. He smiled warmly as he came in from the mezzanine that overlooked the huge lounge and promenade decks of the ship. There was Roberts, a youngster who thought he was going to burn up the universe with his work in transfinite mechanics—but who was looking very downcast now because of his inability to solve their problem. Roberts had good stuff in him, Mayhew knew.

There were also Kesserling and Wabell. Good men, but lacking Roberts' imagination.

"What's the trouble?" said Mayhew. "Have you found anything?"

Roberts shook his head dolefully. "I guess we ought to be back in some service shop repairing televisors. For all we know about transfinite mechanics we could—"

"Don't worry," said Mayhew. "Better men have been stumped by easier problems. Do you know where you are?"

Roberts shook his head. "I thought I had it figured out, but we're lost, that's all. In fact, I don't even think we're in the right C any more."

"If you had the courage to follow through on some of your guesses you'd hit the right answer more often," said Mayhew. "That's exactly what happened. You went into C° and have been wandering around there. All your responses have been to other C sets instead of to Aleph sets as you thought. That's why your indications have been all jumbled up. We've got to go back into the C set first and then to the Aleph."

"How can we locate our own C? Is there any characteristic by which we can identify it?"

"We don't have to. They are all alike. There is a C set of identical C's. Anyone of them will do."

"Hey, wait a minute," said Wabell. "We want to get back to our own good old terra firma, not some reasonably exact facsimile thereof."

Mayhew grinned. "I guess the human mind will never become adjusted to thinking in terms of transfinities. When we fix ourselves into one C set, the whole multiplicity of them will appear as unity, just as is the case with the Alephs. So we'll be in our right one, you don't need to worry about that."

Wabell frowned, then threw his hands up in despair. "I wasn't cut out for this kind of stuff. Give me some tubes and transformers and a little juice to shoot through them and I can tell you what'll happen, but this—"

"—is all done with tubes and transformers and juice," said Mayhew, "plus a little unconventional math. The trouble is that math terms are the only ones that can be used to speak of the transfinite. Once you try to describe it in any other language, you're lost in a morass of inaccurate semantic jumbling that conveys no meaning. But let's be on our way back. Is the equipment working so that you can pass down to C?"

Roberts nodded. "I'll have the equations set up in a moment. How about your ship?"

"The Raft? It's tied onto the *Express* so it'll tag along. Go ahead. Let's see you get us down a notch."

Then Mayhew turned to Captain Drangue. "Better warn the passengers. This is rather unpleasant." He described the lower set, and Drangue nodded, stepping to the ship's communicator to carry out the request. He was barely through with the announcement when the vast prairie of light and flowing coruscations began to fade.

'The congealed gray fog began to reappear, blinding the occupants of the *Express* to anything that might be outside. And as the stuff began to grow fluid and sweep by in great undulations of thickening darkness and light, it seemed that they might be at the bottom of a vast and infinite sea.

Mayhew could imagine the effect on some of the more sensitive female passengers down in the lounge as they gazed out upon that blind, impalpable waste. He was glad he wasn't down there right now.

"One more step and we'll be home," he said. "Hold it a minute, Roberts. I want to call Jack Sebastian at the Terminal and let him know we're coming in. Things weren't going so well there when I left. Some of the more irate citizens were about to take the Terminal apart because the *Express* was late."

He put through the call and watched the face of Jack Sebastian materializing on the screen. He looked sleepy and bored.

"Sebastian," he answered as the call came. "Who? Hey, Chief! I didn't recognize you for a minute. I thought you were home asleep hours ago. What's up?"

"Asleep!" What are you talking about? I've found the *Express* and I'm bringing it in. Is everything all right there?"

"The *Express?*" Sebastian's face wrinkled incredulity. "What *Express* are you talking about?"

MAYHEW swore ponderously to himself. The operations chief must have found the suspense too much and gone out for a bottle.

"Look, Jack," he said patiently. The *Tantalus Express* didn't arrive tonight. It was lost in the *interim*. I left in the Raft and located it. I am now ready to bring it in. I want to know if everything is all right there to set it down in the landing cradle."

"Chief, listen—" Sebastian's face was pitiful now. "The *Express came* in—the *Tantalus Express*—it's been here for two hours. Look, you can see it out there now!"

Sebastian moved away from the panel so that Mayhew could glimpse beyond the windows of the Operations room to the lighted area outside.

And the *Express was* there.

Its lights were out and the huge ship lay motionless and silent as Mayhew had seen it so many times before. There was no mistaking it. The luxury liner was the only one of its kind.

"Chief, I don't get the gag," said Sebastian miserably.

"Jack," Mayhew answered in a low voice, "something's wrong. I don't know what it is, but there's something terribly wrong."

His words, and the tone of his voice, sent faint chills along the spines of those listening in the control room of the *Express*.

"Tell me if the Raft is there," said Mayhew.

"Sure it's here. You just finished it up. It hasn't been tried, even…"

Mayhew turned away, his face utterly white. Roberts swallowed hard and opened his mouth to speak, then closed it silently. Drangue looked from one to the other in blank astonishment.

There was just one final horror to be encountered.

Mayhew spoke slowly into the communicator. "Jack, I want you to call my apartment on another line and see if there is any answer."

Sebastian obeyed without questioning. Mayhew turned aside to glance at Kesserling and Wabell. They were both in a complete funk.

Then Sebastian was back. There was the same kind of incomprehension on his face as was mirrored on Roberts'. "Mayhew!" he cried. "If this is some kind of a joke I think it's gone far enough. I don't, get it!"

"Who answered at my apartment?"

"You did, of course."

Mayhew slumped visibly.

Sebastian was saying, "I can see you in both screens, Chief. Tell me what this is all about!"

"Let me talk to…" Mayhew glanced wearily about. "…to myself," he said.

Sebastian hesitated an instant, then made the connection. Instantly there appeared a pajama-clad figure, who was staring incredulously out at the men in the control room of the *Express.* And the man was Mayhew.

After a moment be chuckled. "I've seen some neat gags in my time, but this tops 'em. What goes on?"

"Tell me quickly—did the *Tantalus Express* come in on schedule tonight without any indication of trouble?"

"Of course. There was no trouble."

"You have the Raft ready for use?"

"Yes. What do you know about the Raft?"

"Plenty. But there's only one way of convincing you of what I know and who I am. Will you come to me on the Raft so that we can figure out exactly what is wrong?"

"As far as I know nothing is wrong. Would you mind telling me who you are and what is the idea of this gag?"

"It's no gag. Do you realize who I am?"

"That's what I'm asking."

"I'm Carl Mayhew."

"And I'm Napoleon…"

"Tonight the *Tantalus Express* was missing. I went on a search trip in the Raft and found it in C°. I called back to check before bringing the ship in—and I find, you, or rather *me,* telling myself that the *Express* was never missing."

The second Mayhew chuckled again. "Amusing, but not quite convincing. Suppose you tell me just what you expect in return for this entertainment."

Mayhew cursed. But he couldn't blame the duplicate. That's the way *he* would act, confronted by such an impossible situation.

"There's only one thing to do," he said. "Come to me on the Raft for a conference. You can follow our guide beam here. I'll give you the figures when you get to the Terminal."

The smile left the face of the second Mayhew as the conviction came that he was talking with someone who knew transfinite operations. But the story of a missing *Express* in which *he* was supposed to be right now was too absurd.

"I don't know who you are or what your game is," he said slowly, "but I think I'll come out and see just how far this goes. If there's any monkey business I warn you you'll regret it."

"Stop being stupid! There's no time to lose. Get down to the Terminal and see if you can pick up my guide beam."

"I'm coming, and I'll remember that crack."

In the control room of the *Tantalus Express* there was an absolute silence, as Mayhew turned slowly to the others.

CHAPTER FOUR
Ulysses of the Stars

THE ALARM sounded. The five men straightened as if it were the clarion of some frightful ghost whose coming they waited, yet whose existence they could not credit.

"He's contacted the guide beam," said Mayhew. "Maybe that will convince him."

"Maybe it will convince us," said Roberts.

Mayhew switched on the communicator again and found himself looking into the control pit of the Raft—or at least *a* Raft. And there was his own image, more serious and thoughtful than before.

"I didn't believe it," the second Mayhew said. "I thought it was some crackpot practical joke, but there is a guide beam and it goes somewhere across the transfinite. Let me have those figures you mentioned, mister. I'm coming to visit you."

Mayhew grinned wryly and read off the settings that would enable the Raft to penetrate the C° region. Then he set the guide to bring the Raft up to the *Express* on the side opposite the first Raft.

"Come ahead," he said.

The panel image vanished instantly, and Roberts, looking out the port, exclaimed, "He's here! Mayhew, there's another Raft out there!"

Mayhew glanced at Drangue. "Get him, will you? I don't think it would be a good idea for the passengers to see the two of us together just now."

Drangue nodded and walked out.

No one spoke while the captain was gone. Mayhew stepped to the wide port and stared out into the impenetrable fog that was neither matter nor energy but only a blanking out of the senses as they failed to respond to the world of C in which the ship lay.

He was roused by a voice that sounded irritatingly sardonic, "Mr. Mayhew, I presume?"

He recognized it as his own voice, and turned slowly. The sudden, shocked expression that came over the face of the newcomer told the story of the mental conflicts within him.

"I didn't believe it… Now I've got to," he said at last.

The man was Mayhew, to the last, tiniest detail.

"Are you really convinced now?" said Mayhew.

The newcomer sat down slowly and nodded. "I'm trying to tell myself I'm still back there dreaming and I'll wake up in the morning and forget all about this. Whatever it is— however you came to be here—bring me up to date."

"First, we ought to decide who's who. Suppose we call me Mayhew-a and you Mayhew-b. Would that be satisfactory?"

"It makes no difference to me. I wonder, though, who came first, a or b?"

"That's the nub of the whole problem. But here's the way it is—"

Mayhew-a quickly outlined his experiences and his attempts to bring the *Express* back to Earth.

"Is there none of that that fits your own experience pattern?" he concluded.

Mayhew-b shook his head. "Not a thing. It's just as I told you before. The *Express* came in on time. All the passengers were present and unharmed. There was no indication whatever of anything wrong. The passengers and crew have disembarked and the ship is lying empty except for the maintenance crew readying it for the next trip."

"Well, we won't find the answer by talking about it. It must lie somewhere in the transfinite equations covering our presence here." He moved over to the giant calculator and sat down in front of it.

Rapidly, he set up the classical transfinite expressions governing the transport of an object from Aleph-Null to C.

"Now," he said, "what happens when we introduce a finite t into these expressions, instead of an infinitesimal time period?"

"Nothing," said Mayhew-b. "The expressions you have there do not govern a static condition but only the transient condition between departure and arrival. They become meaningless if you try to interpret any point on the curve as a static condition."

"Yes. I remember Hooper tried to develop such an expression and got nowhere with it. But how about the work that Rodney did? He developed a meaningful expression for C containing an element of N."

"It was never verified, though. If you expect to tackle this mathematically—and I admit there is no other way—you're attacking a problem that's baffled the best transfinite men for the last decade."

"What else would you suggest?"

"Nothing. Put down Rodney's expression below yours and solve them simultaneously for the N element. That ought to show you if the element will be duplicated. Then maybe we can find out what will happen to it when it is brought back to N."

Mayhew-a nodded. That was a good attack. His fingers danced upon the keys of the calculator and slowly the ponderous expressions appeared.

While they worked, oblivious to their surroundings, Roberts and the two other technicians sat silently and motionlessly, watching the work that would decide their fate and that of every person aboard the ship. Once, Roberts wanted to inject a thought as he glimpsed the intent of the manipulation that Mayhew-a was performing, but the work passed so swiftly before his eyes that the point was lost and he sat back, envying the swift flow of mathematical thought that was emerging from the minds of the duplicate engineers like crystals born in the hot fires of some cataclysm.

Roberts knew Mayhew with some degree of intimacy, and he was accustomed to seeing the chief working calmly without strain, producing intricate mathematical structures that seemed to leap into being almost of themselves. But now Mayhew-a was tight-lipped and stress lines were in his face. Only Mayhew-b was calm and unworried. Regardless of outward similarity, there was surely a difference in the two men, Roberts thought. Mayhew-b was more like the old, confident, sure Mayhew.

MAYHEW-a suddenly observed an error far back in his manipulations and angrily wiped the board clean, then began over, piling up the incomprehensible structure of transfinite conceptions that would explain the presence of the duplications.

But shortly, Mayhew-b stopped him and pointed out another error he had just made.

"We won't get anywhere this way," said Mayhew-b. "We need a slight drink."

"Drink? Not now—"

"Remember how we clinched the final dope that made the Raft tick? Two weeks of solid, bone-dry working without success, and then just one little Tantalus Special did the trick. Remember?"

Mayhew-a suddenly grinned and relaxed. "Okay, pal, you win. Let's go."

The Mayhews rose, linked arms, and went out the door. Drangue watched them go with an exasperated scowl. But Roberts had brightened perceptibly. "We'll get results now," he said. "That's the way it goes with Mayhew. I've seen him stew until he comes to a slow boil, then he tells the whole business to go to the devil and goes out for a drink. When he comes back, he's got it. That's Mayhew. Let's go down and have one on the house."

Drangue shrugged and followed him out. He had become convinced that this ship would be their eternal tomb.

The Mayhews made their way toward the bar, passing along the promenade deck.

Mayhew-a observed the increasing stares. "We'd better say you are my twin."

"Why? Let 'em think they're drunk."

When the first Trans-Astra ships began to cross unbelievable spans of the void in an instant, something became lacking in space travel. Hence, aboard the *Express* the instant of time required for travel was distorted—for most, the illusion of a week's journey to Tantalus made a satisfactory trip.

In the bar the light was pleasantly diffuse and subdued. A dozen other people were seated about the room.

Mayhew-a was well into his second Tantalus Special, and Mayhew-b was beginning his fourth—evidently the differences in their recent lines had produced many temperamental dissimilarities when their thoughts were interrupted by the arrival of a couple who came up next to them at the bar. It was Susan Dawning and a companion.

"I didn't know you were twins, Mr. Mayhew," said Susan. "Or am I seeing double?"

"No, there are really two of us. Identical twins. This is my brother, Mr. Mayhew."

Mayhew-b nodded enthusiastically. "Identical twins— that's right. Have a slug of dishwater on us? Who's your friend?"

Susan Dawning introduced them to James Darrell, the author, and he was obviously neither charmed nor delighted to see either Mayhew, though he said he was.

"This all seems rather thrilling," said Susan. "I think it would help business if the company arranged for every ship to get lost. These trips become so boring."

Mayhew-a growled his dislike for people who were eternally "thrilled."

"Suppose we don't get back at all," he said. "Would that be thrilling, too?"

"Well, hardly. But I'm sure there's not the slightest chance of that with Mr. Mayhew, the great scientist, taking care of us."

Then her eyes clouded with puzzlement. "But which one of you *is* Mr. Mayhew, the scientist?"

"He is," said both Mayhews simultaneously.

Before Susan Dawning could reply, one of the emcees came in from the adjacent lounge and spoke to her. "They're asking for you to come back and sing. They are some of the most unstable ones that Warren is concerned about. He thinks you're good for them."

"Of course, John. I should have known better than to leave."

The girl left her glass on the bar and followed the emcee into the next lounge. Mayhew-a paid no attention until he noticed his companion watching Susan intently.

"Let's go in and hear her," said Mayhew-b. "I've always liked her singing and acting, bat I've never heard her in person before."

Mayhew-a scowled. "That torch singer? She hasn't got the slightest suggestion of a brain. This is all just a 'thrill' to her and a chance for more publicity. Didn't you bear what she said?"

"It's funny," said Mayhew-b, slowly. "Now I never suspected myself of being neurotic. Getting a look at yourself reveals things—"

"Who's neurotic?"

"You're taking things entirely too seriously."

"I just said that—"

"I know."

"Well, what's that got to do with it?"

"Miss Dawning seems to me to be a very competent and stable young woman," said Mayhew-b. "Let's hear her sing."

They wandered towards the doorway into the lounge where sixty or seventy of the passengers were gathered. Susan had already begun her song. As Mayhew-a watched the passengers he could understand Warren's intense concern. Telltale lines of worry and fear were upon their faces. Here was the nucleus of panic that could sweep the ship disastrously.

But as the girl sang, he saw the lines of tension and fear relax somewhat.

This was a typical cross section of the passenger group. A dozen businessmen on vacation, students, playboys, one or two old couples on anniversary trips.

Somehow, Mayhew-a observed the girl had the ability to reach them all. Her clear soprano voice had good musical quality, far different from that of many of her competitors. He watched the face of Mayhew-b, as Susan sang.

The other's face was lighted with enthusiasm and when she finished he clapped loudly. "That girl's got something," he said, "Did you watch the faces of those people as she sang? She's got something!"

BACK in the control room all traces of inebriety in Mayhew-b vanished. He frowned as he watched the steady stream of metamorphosing equations pour forth under the fingers of Mayhew-a. Complicated transformations of transfinite expressions spread unintelligible configurations before them.

"Nowhere do you see an expression for a duplicate member of a set which has revolved through the *interim* and returned to its original set," said Mayhew-b.

"You know," said Mayhew-a, "this *could* mean that all of our past understanding of transfinite processes with respect to the operation of these ships has been fallacious. We've never really been sure of our interpretation anyway—in spite of what we've confidently told the public.

"So? Then what is the correct interpretation?"

"Suppose that the set *you* belong to is not the one from which this *Express* originated. These two elements originated in different Aleph-Nulls. Then it's possible that something was wrong and is still wrong, preventing this ship from getting back to its own Aleph-Null."

"Then that would mean that you and I are not exactly duplicates, but individuals—and likewise for every other element of our set. It doesn't make sense."

"Wait a minute. Actually, there's no reality in the thing we're talking about—at least from the Aleph-Null viewpoint. But we know that from the Aleph-Null viewpoint all the sets of Aleph-Null appear as unity, just as in C all the sets of C appear as one. But from here we can understand that an Aleph-Null number of Aleph-Null sets exists, and in each of them are a Carl Mayhew and a *Tantalus Express* undergoing simultaneous and duplicate experiences.

"But suppose, now, that these Aleph Null number of *Express* ships left the Aleph-Null number of Tantaluses and started for their own Earths—suppose that one of them, this one, got sidetracked and couldn't find the way back to its own Aleph-Null set. So when I call you, expecting to find a place waiting for us, I find that one of the other ships has already landed there."

"That would mean that somewhere there is an Aleph-Null set without an *Express*—and without a Carl Mayhew, or any of these other people—"

"Right. Hence the problem is still that of the needle in an infinity of haystacks, finding the one Aleph-Null set that does not have an *Express*."

"No—no—" Mayhew-b suddenly stood up and strode around the room, thrusting his fingers through his hair. "Even if it happened that way, the guide beam from that particular Aleph-Null set would be reaching out and we could follow it in."

"Not necessarily. An Aleph-Null number of guide beams have been turned off. Subtract Aleph-Null from Aleph-Null and you get anything from zero to Aleph-Null. In this case you apparently get zero for some reason or other."

"The whole idea is nuts. Suppose it happened that way. You were back in your Aleph-Null of which there was only one perceptible because all the Aleph-Null sets registered as unity. All right, there were still an Aleph-Null number of *Expresses* distributed among the Alephs in the C set, so that from the Aleph-Null viewpoint all *Expresses* were present and accounted for."

"Uh-huh," said Mayhew-a "except that you are forgetting the one *Express* that was in C°."

"So what? Aleph-Null minus one is still Aleph-Null."

"If you follow that to its logical conclusion then we *are* extra and there is no Aleph-Null set to which we can return. Maybe what happened was equivalent to adding one to the set of Aleph-Null number of universes in which the transfer took place."

"Couldn't do. That would make it a separate and distinct entity, no longer possessing congruency with the other sets of Aleph-Null."

"Maybe that's why we can't find it. Somewhere there is this unique set with zero *Expresses*. And while, as Peano showed centuries ago, zero is a number, it is unique in having no predecessor. That fact would render this particular set unique."

"No. That's impossible. If it happened in one Aleph-Null set it would happen to all. There is no event that can be unique to one number of a set in that manner."

"I fail to see why not. You just stated yourself that the subtraction of one unit would not alter the cardinality of the set. But what happens to this subtracted unit? It's got to continue in existence."

"Ah—there you have it, my boy," said Mayhew-b in ponderous tones. "State in exact, semantically exact terms, the meaning of existence."

"Yeah," said Mayhew-a dourly. "I know what you mean. But we still haven't gotten anywhere."

They dropped into silence; then Mayhew-b said, "Frankly, I'm convinced there's no way out of it. I think I'm going to have to put up with you for the rest of my life. But don't think I'm going to split my pay check with you."

"Your paycheck! Now just who works for Trans-Astra?"

"That should make a neat problem."

"The situation is impossible."

"Right. But there's not a thing to do about it. We've got an extra ship. Perhaps there's a set minus one. If so, we'll never find it. Regardless, the only thing is for us to go back and take up our duplicate existences. We can't spend the rest of our lives out here, and you know perfectly well we'll never find the mythical set that is minus its *Express*."

"It'd ruin Trans-Astra. The question of splitting our—my paycheck would be insignificant. How about Governor Wesson, for example? He comes back and finds there's already a Governor Wesson occupying his office—not to mention his bed and board. What would his wife do with two husbands? In some cases the doubles might decide the world wasn't big enough to hold both of them. Take that guy Jeff Wicks, for example. His two halves would probably kill each other off."

"No loss."

"Maybe not. But a big stink. And how about two Susan Dawnings?"

"Now, brother, you're talking. I'm going to call Jack Sebastian and break the news about this business to him gently—unless you have objections?"

Mayhew-a waved away the question. He was sick of the whole incomprehensible problem. He knew they couldn't take all these duplicated people back to Earth. Yet what else was there to do? Anyway it wouldn't hurt to let Mayhew-b wrestle with the problem for a while.

In a moment the screen lighted and the face of Jack Sebastian appeared. He recognized Mayhew. "Hello, Chief. What's up?"

"I'm coming back—eventually, but there's—ah—a problem you should know about—"

"Back? Where've you been? I thought you said you were going to get a load of shuteye tonight."

The sudden silence within the control room of the *Express* was unbearable. The two Mayhews looked at each other and Mayhew-b grew visibly paler. He turned again to the panel in fear and exasperation.

" Jack, don't you remember?" he demanded. "I took the Raft out to C to look for the missing *Tantalus Express*."

"I don't get this doubletalk, Chief. The express came in and the Raft is here—" Mayhew; broke the connection.

"Now *you're* it," said Mayhew.

CHAPTER FIVE
Tantalus

FOR A long time the Mayhews sat there looking at their equations and their fingers.

"Funny, isn't it?" said Mayhew-b at last. "It makes you kind of homesick to think you can't ever get back to your own set, to the exact place and circumstances you've known all your life."

"Don't get lost in a bunch of non-semantic nonsense. You know that statement has absolutely no meaning."

"And again, what is *meaning?*"

"Cut it out! Anyway, I think one of my points is illustrated. Our contact between here and the Alephs is absolutely random. We are likely to pick anyone of an Aleph-Null number of worlds. So the one you came from and the one I came from are not the same—"

"From the C viewpoint that is true, but they are the same from the Aleph-Null viewpoint, remember."

"No. There's a difference somewhere. It's obvious from the fact that the *Express* was missing from my set and not from yours."

They were silent again for a long time, each considering his responsibility toward the twenty-five hundred persons aboard the *Express*.

Mayhew-b felt considerably sobered. Regardless of the intellectual interest he had previously had in the problem, he had been merely a bystander; the *Express* had been no responsibility of his, because his set was complete. But now the impact of the knowledge that he, too, was a man lost from his own set jolted that attitude from his mind. The problem was a personal one, now.

"Suppose we land on some distant, out-of-the-way planet," he said at last, "and wreck the ship, telling the passengers it was accidental. It might not be so bad starting up a new world that way."

"That may be the only practical answer in the end," said Mayhew-a, "but I don't believe we have the moral right to make the decision. I believe we should try everything else, possible first and then if we still fail we can put the problem up to the people—let them decide if they want to go back and try to live duplicate lives or go to some distant planet."

"Actually, I wonder if we still have any reality. I wonder if we are not just mathematical shadows—"

Their speculations were suddenly broken off by the entrance of Drangue. They had not seen him since they had previously left the control room.

"I've been looking all over for you," said Drangue. "I've just talked with Warren, the psychologist. He says that we've got to get out of here and go to some familiar place, and do it fast. The emotional potential of the passengers has accumulated to some high point on a scale that he has, which means that there's going to be assorted riots, mutiny and general bloodshed if we don't move out of this gray stuff."

"I've been afraid of something like this," said Mayhew-a.

Drangue said, "Warren suggested a return to Tantalus if we can't go back to Earth."

Mayhew-a rose and went outside the control room to the mezzanine overlooking the main lounge and the promenade deck. From where he stood he could see little gatherings of eight or ten persons. He couldn't hear what they were saying, but in their sharp, nervous gestures he could feel the building up of panic. He had sensed it when he first came aboard, and down in the lounge it had been almost unbearable until Susan had quieted it. Now it was ready to spill over and wreak havoc aboard the ship.

He guessed there would be a storming of the control room with seemingly rational demands to know what was going on. Then there would be threats, physical violence, and finally would come general rioting.

He shuddered. Sometimes he wished he had gone more deeply into psychology. Certainly the complexities of the transfinite were no greater than the unknown realms of the human brain.

He returned to the control room. "It looks as if Warren's right. We can go back to Tantalus for a time. Perhaps that would be the most logical thing to do anyway. We can turn them loose among the Pleasure Regions and that should cool them off considerably. In the meantime, we may be able to work this out."

The eyes of Mayhew-b were intent upon his as he uttered the last few words, "I wouldn't count on that too much," said Mayhew-b slowly. "I'm convinced that the problem is insoluble. I'm serious in saying that we'll have to face the facts of our duplicate existence."

"We've got to give ourselves every possible chance to find an answer," said Mayhew-a tensely. "We haven't done that, yet. Drangue, make the necessary announcements to the passengers. Tell them we have made sufficient repairs or something to enable us to return to Tantalus. Tell them that we will complete the work there and return to Earth as soon as possible."

There was a silence.

Dubiously, Drangue moved to do as he was bidden.

TANTALUS!

In scarlet letters the name stood out in space like a great neon sign a hundred thousand miles across. And it revolved slowly about the planet like the rings of Saturn.

The creation of Tantalus was the work of an interstellar council on recreation. It had come to the attention of the governments of the worlds that in spite of the social advancement of the past centuries, the supplying of entertainment to the masses of the people was still a haphazard, unscientific and often dangerous process.

And so Tantalus had been built—a scientific dream world to serve the Universe. It was designed on psychological principles to relax and relieve, to fulfill in a socially desirable manner the unsatisfied and unattainable longings of the multitudes who sought its pleasures. A weekend on Tantalus, the Pleasure Planet, was guaranteed to renew the weariest of men.

Slowly, Roberts brought the great ship into the port of Tantalus as Drangue reported their emergency situation to the register clerk. He learned there were about thirty-six hours before the regularly scheduled run of the *Express*.

Mayhew-b looked significantly at Mayhew-a as Drangue reported the time.

"There's your absolute limit. Thirty-six hours. In that time you've got to solve some mathematical problems that haven't been solved in ten years of transfinite travel. It can't be done. And even if it is you don't know what the answer will mean with regard to this misplaced *Express*. Why don't you tell the people the truth? This double existence isn't going to be so bad. I'm even beginning to like you."

"I thought we settled that a while ago. You may like this double existence, but most of these people wouldn't. Come on, let's get busy."

The ship was always brought back to N_0 at a distance from Tantalus, so that the illusion of normal travel and arrival could be maintained. As Roberts lowered the ship into its landing cradle they heard the rumble of the multiple gangways being extended to all levels of the ship for disembarkation. The Mayhews resumed work at the calculator. The other four men in the room remained with them, but the passengers poured from the ship as if fleeing from some unknown horror.

As the hours lengthened and the natural night of the planet approached, it became obvious to both Mayhews that they were getting nowhere in their manipulations. They had succeeded in obtaining a static expression for an N element in C°, but they had been unable to obtain any simultaneous expression for the condition of the N set with one element removed to C°. And it looked very much as if the problem could be shown to be insoluble.

As they sat staring at the meaningless equations, the door of the control room slowly opened. In surprise, they looked up and saw Susan Dawning.

"I hope I'm not intruding," she said softly.

"I'm afraid you are," said Mayhew-a. "We're very busy. Will you please leave?"

"Just a minute," said Mayhew-b. He rose and extended a hand to Susan. "My brother's temper is a bit short today. We've been having a slight struggle with this broken-down buggy we're aboard. What can we do for you?"

"I don't know anything about the tremendous complexities of what you are doing," said Susan. "But I am aware that something extremely unusual has gone wrong— something you haven't quite told us the whole truth about. Am I right?"

Mayhew-b nodded slowly. "You are very perceptive, but—"

"In which case the fate of all of us depends upon your finding the answer to the difficulty. You've been working steadily for six hours since we landed. I don't believe even your brains are capable of working efficiently at such a pace much longer. So I'm inviting you to take a little time off and join me in one of the Pleasure Regions—and perhaps dinner after. For the good of all of us aboard the *Express*, you understand."

Mayhew-a began an answer that turned into a muffled explosion as Mayhew-b cut him off. "That would be an excellent idea," the latter said. "I was just thinking that our brains had about ground themselves down to a slow stop. What do you say?"

Mayhew-a made no answer for a moment, then he slapped the release key of the calculator board in a gesture of admitted defeat and rose. Their last two hours had been absolutely futile.

He nodded. "I guess we need it all right. Come on, you guys." He beckoned to the captain and the technicians whose silent presence he had almost forgotten. "Let's knock off for a while."

Outside, Susan said, "I don't know how in the world anyone ever tells you Mayhews apart. I wouldn't have the slightest idea whether I was talking to Mayhew the scientist, or Mayhew the—"

"Mathematician," said Mayhew-b. "But it isn't necessary to tell us apart. One will do about as well as the other in most cases."

"Except love."

"What?"

"Didn't you ever fall in love? It would then make a difference as to who's who."

"We're the bachelor type," said Mayhew-a. "Strictly the bachelor type."

SUSAN made no comment until they reached the checking center. I thought we might go to the Music of the Spheres Region," she said. "Would you care for that?"

"That'd be fine," said Mayhew-b. "But we'll have to get a psych-check first. They might not permit it."

"Do I have to be checked again? I was just here."

"Yes. It's required every time you come."

A continuous stream of people was moving along the walks towards the psychological checking center, the only mundane note on the whole planet. Here each applicant for entrance into the Regions of Pleasure was checked mentally and physically, advised as to the regions he could enter with most benefit and prohibited from any activity that would be harmful. The checking was entirely impersonal and automatic. A machine made a rapid analysis of the brainwave patterns, and rendered a form verdict based upon the analysis.

As the Mayhews came out of the checking booths they noted the list of activities approved for each of them. They had identical special analyses, a service rendered in particularly difficult cases.

It read: "Extreme tension exists as the result of conflicting drives, whose resolution appears as an insoluble problem. Psychiatric procedure advised. Advisable Pleasure Region sequence as follows: First day: Music of the Spheres, forty-five minutes; Gardens of Delight, optional time; Cafe of Heaven.

"Nice program they have outlined for us," said Mayhew-b. "I wouldn't mind going through the whole thing. It would probably do us some good. Apparently, we're more than slightly neurotic according to this analysis."

"Yes, but the program is laid out for a whole week and we only have thirty hours to stay here."

Inside the building housing the entrance to the Music of the Spheres Region, they were assigned dressing rooms where they donned the briefest of costumes to allow them the benefit of the radiation in the Region. Then they stepped onto the escalator leading up to the takeoff dais.

As they stood in line before the takeoff tube, Susan was first with Mayhew-b, and Mayhew-a, behind her. Watching his companions, Mayhew-a decided that there could be no mistaking their response to each other. It was becoming intensified with every passing moment. And it mystified him. Mayhew-b couldn't rationally consider the attraction of the actress as more than sheer biology. There was no question of her attractiveness from that viewpoint.

But she lived in a world that didn't exist for Mayhew-b, and she could never hope to gain any adequate conception of his. Her attitude towards men was certainly neurotic, considering the number of times her highly publicized romances had nearly—but not quite—culminated in marriage.

He didn't understand it.

Abruptly, they were at the head of the line. Susan stepped into the transparent, cylindrical chamber at the end of the platform. She put her arms above her head and waved gaily to them. Then she was gone as she shot upward with incredible speed into the pink light that bathed her from overhead.

The light vanished and Mayhew-b stepped into the chamber. The process was repeated and he likewise vanished upward. Finally, Mayhew-a stepped in.

He extended his arms above his head as the others had done. He glanced momentarily upward at the endless expanse that stretched above him, merging with the space in the cylinder until the cylinder appeared no more. Then suddenly the pink light flashed about him and he was soaring upward.

There was just an instant of vertigo; then it was gone and he was soaring upward on godlike wings into a vague, enormous space. There was light here, diffuse and without source, as if it were a property of space itself. As he sped onward, the pink deepened and he felt the beneficent rays tingling against his skin, renewing his energies.

There was no sign of his companions, for a moment he drifted in solitude, his mind at peace. There were no bounds to the infinite depths about him. And in this world of light and endless space there were myriad, multi-hued spheres rotating and dancing about at random, like planets that had escaped the laws of celestial mechanics. He darted headlong towards one of the globes. It remained stationary until he was almost upon it and then it soared upwards and away, at the same time emitting a tinkling of elfin music from its depths.

He did not pursue the elusive sphere, but continued his headlong flight. Shortly the pink began to dim and darken and he found himself entering a region tinged with green. It was pleasant and soothing. He slowed his mad plunging through space and spiraled slowly into the depths of the green region until the color darkened like the depths of the sea.

Here in this quiet seclusion he came to rest and the waves of sudden music burst upon his senses. Low and almost inaudible at first, there was the sound as of some mighty, distant organ and he recognized the sound of its music: "The Sunken Bell."

He closed his eyes and rested, motionless and without burden in that sea-green space, and as the organ notes mounted to crescendo they burst over him with great waves of sound that rocked him with their might, bathing and cleansing his soul of its cares.

An eternity later the peaceful music broke into raw minor chords that roused him from his lethargy. Slowly but insistently, it impelled him to soar onward and seek other regions.

WITHOUT regret he resumed his flight, and presently came to an area of yellow where flaming fire seemed to hang in the space about him. The sourceless light flamed and died and burned bright again, challenging, exhilarating.

Many darting figures were visible now and he suddenly found himself near his companions. They were toying with the spheres, soaring after them amidst the thunderous, triumphal music that washed over them.

He watched Susan. Like a slim goddess in the sky she was hurtling above him in pursuit of a silver globe, and, suddenly triumphant, she seized it and bore it aloft in her outstretched hands, arcing through the heavens like Diana with her moon globe.

Impulsively, Mayhew-a sped after a flaming sun globe. It leaped ahead of him like a living thing, and its fiery prominences lashed out at him. Willing himself to a titanic burst of speed, he caught the sun, and hurled it across the vault of space where Mayhew-b soared.

Mayhew-b caught the flaming sphere and darted exultantly after the moon-goddess, Susan.

In contrast to the world of sea-quiet peace that Mayhew-a had left, this was a world of flame and violent motion where men were gods, at once omnipotent and all wise.

Then Mayhew-a watched the image of his duplicate soar in the heights where Susan's flight had carried her. Mayhew-b snatched away the silver globe and darted downward.

Instantly, Susan swooped after him, as if she were Diana in pursuit of Apollo.

She caught up with Mayhew-b, and flung her arms about him in a wild, exultant embrace. And time seemed to stand still for Mayhew-a, as he watched the flight of the two figures. Mayhew-b like some fallen god hurtling head downward towards a flaming purgatory, bearing the treacherous goddess who laughingly clung to him.

CHAPTER SIX
The Face of Terror

THAT evening calamity struck as the three dined in the Cafe of Heaven. The menu was that prepared for those who had visited the Music of the Spheres Region and the Gardens of Delight. It was scientifically concocted to carry out the physical and psychological processes begun by these entertainment regions.

While they ate, they watched a three-dimensional televised show broadcast from Earth. Mayhew-a watched it without attention until a sudden announcement startled him to alertness.

"Our next number is sung by the darling of the airscreens. We give you Susan Dawning!"

Instantly, a lifelike image of Susan Dawning appeared in the center of a bubble of light projected in the middle of the room. A song began in the well-known voice of Susan. It was a plaintive song about some forgotten love. But the first words were scarcely uttered when Susan stood up between the Mayhews and exclaimed, "That's an impostor! *I'm* Susan Dawning!"

Oblivious to the interruption, the image went on, but every eye in the room turned towards the figure in white who strode towards the center of the room and slapped her hand through the immaterial image.

"Stop this!" she demanded of the entertainment director, who came running forward to see what the trouble was.

Mayhew-a groaned audibly. "The fat's in the fire." Then he looked at Mayhew-b. *"You* get it out," he said meaningly.

"Me? Why me?"

"Heaven only knows. But you've got the power. I didn't miss that scene in the Region. Get going before the whole thing is tumbling down on our heads."

Mayhew-b nodded and slipped away to the center of confusion about the still singing televised figure.

He grasped her arm. "It's probably only a recording, Susan. Don't you recognize one of your own records?"

"Recording! I've never made one. All my appearances have been personal. I'll sue this—this—"

She stopped and gazed in horrified fascination at the singing form. The eyes, the hair, every gesture—and then she began singing in unison while the crowd in the Cafe stared in bewilderment at the twin figures singing their strange duet, one real, one an image of light.

When it was done, Susan said in a small voice, "It's *me*. Carl, it is. How—"

She stared past him to Mayhew-a sitting like a stone image at the table they had left. Her gaze returned to Mayhew-b and her hand suddenly raised to her mouth to cut off a sharp exclamation of horror. "No, Carl! That isn't what's happened—"

"Come on, Susan, please. We will give you all the explanations we have. Please come quickly and let's not make any more disturbance."

As if sleepwalking, she allowed herself to be led back to the table to Mayhew-a. Then, before any of them had a chance to speak, a new blast exploded in their midst. As the image of Susan Dawning finished another song, an announcer appeared.

"We have a news bulletin, ladies and gentlemen, reporting the tragic death of beloved Calvert Mason, well known philanthropist and Director of Semantic Relations at the Universal Embassy. Mr. Mason's body was found in the library of his home this afternoon with a knife wound in the back. His nephew, Jeffry Wicks, is being held and has confessed to the murder, explaining that Mason had cut him out of his will and refused to give him any more money for gambling debts. Not only tragic because it brought death to Mr. Mason, but because it is the first instance of murder in over a decade—"

Across the room a sudden hurricane of confusion began as Calvert Mason jumped to his feet and exclaimed, "What sort of preposterous nonsense is this?"

"Let's get out of here," whispered Mayhew-a hoarsely. "We've got to get everyone aboard the ship and leave Tantalus."

"Carl—" Susan's face was white.

"Darling, there's just no time to explain now," said Mayhew-b.

They made their hurried exit from the building and ran along the gaily-lighted ways that led to the ship. When they reached the control room of the *Express* Drangue was already there in a heated argument with Roberts.

"Mayhew!" Roberts exclaimed. "Am I glad you showed up! This—this trolley man insists that we should simply take off for Earth in the usual manner now that we're here. I've been trying to convince him that's wrong, but he insisted he was going to do it in spite of you."

Drangue reddened and looked flustered. "I didn't say that—exactly. I said this situation is no different than any of the hundreds of other times that we've been here ready to take off for Earth."

"Look, Drangue," said Mayhew-a evenly. "It is different. Take my word for it if you can't figure it out for yourself, but the existence of us two Mayhews ought to convince you. On the Earth that belongs to this set there is a duplicate of each of us. We just saw the duplicate Susan and we just heard a news flash that Jeff Wicks killed Calvert Mason—the Wicks and Mason on Earth, that is. The noncongruency of events is beginning to catch up with us."

"Then what are we to do?" pleaded Drangue. "We just can *not* go back."

"For the time being I want you to issue a call for every passenger and crew member to report back immediately and we'll take off as soon as they're all aboard."

"For where?"

"We'll tell you later. Tell them the ship has been repaired and we are ready I to take them to—their destination."

The Mayhews left Drangue to carry out the orders and sought an isolated spot in the ship. There, they stood looking out over the vast expanse of buildings containing or leading to the various regions of pleasure. The passengers began to stream back towards the *Express* as Drangue's message went out.

"About Susan," Mayhew-a said suddenly.

Mayhew-b turned slowly. "What about Susan?" he said.

"It's—well, it's just not *Mayhew.*"

Mayhew-b looked out over the city, then back at Mayhew-a. "It's going to be hard for us to get along in some ways. Probably the best thing for us to do will be to separate. We're always going to be figuring out what the other guy ought to say and think and do. But it can't be so. We've split like Siamese twins and our differing experiences will eventually produce two entirely different human beings. What I'm getting at is that while Susan may be a pain in the neck to you, I—well, I'm going to ask her to marry me when and if we get out of this mess. To point out that she has proved herself the sanest one aboard this ship, that she has exhibited more stability and intelligence than any girl I've—we've—met before would be superfluous. Nor is it necessary to present psychological explanations for her highly publicized career in the past, though they exist quite adequately. In short, falling in love has never required an excuse, so I'm afraid the subject is just sort of taboo between us from now on. See what I mean?"

"Yeah—I see what you mean. You are different. Well, good luck, pal."

"Thanks."

THE PASSENGERS were streaming back now, some eager to get aboard in the belief that Drangue's message meant they were leaving for home, some reluctant to enter the ship of fear again. The Mayhews wondered what the reaction would be when the exact nature of their situation was revealed and each person knew that he would have to live in the universe with his duplicate.

They heard a sudden step behind them and Roberts found them in the semidarkness by the window.

"I've been looking all over for you. I want to show you something after our little argument with Drangue. I think I've found a clue to the way out."

"Let's see." Mayhew-a took the papers that Roberts waved excitedly. He scanned the transfinite equations.

"It's like this," said Roberts. "I've been trying to figure out why we were still duplicated when we landed on Tantalus. We know that we are in one of the Aleph-Null sets where we should fit in. Theoretically, since N_0 plus one is still N_0 we should not be duplicates now."

Mayhew-b shook his head. "Your reasoning is wrong. We have just been thrashing out another point based on the same fact—the fact that divergent experience has destroyed our one-to-one correspondence."

"I know. After thinking about it I could see it was absurd to think that merely coming down to an Aleph-Null set would suddenly combine elements seventeen thousand light years apart. It would be a question of who would combine with whom, and how would they get together over that span of space, and a lot of other impossible considerations."

"Right."

"Okay. But now look. What would happen if we reversed our time coordinates to the exact instant when the other *Express* landed at the Terminal after the original departure from Tantalus—what would happen if at that precise instant, we also returned to the Terminal?"

For a moment the Mayhews stared at the young technician in silence. At last Mayhew-b said, "I don't know. Do your equations indicate an answer?"

"Yes. They indicate a reduction of Aleph Null to unity in the Aleph-Null set."

"That's to be expected."

"No, it isn't. Look what happens when we leave out the congruence of time and spatial relationship. That's what we have right now in our landing on Tantalus. We have gone into another Aleph set not identical with any previously known. It had to be that way because this set just didn't exist previously with duplicates in it. Our coming has created a whole new universe!"

"Let me see those figures..." Both Mayhews bent over the sheets intently in the dim light and pondered the equations and their tremendous implications. It certainly looked as if Roberts' work was pointing the way out.

Mayhew-a finally said, "It's worth a try. We can't lose."

"How about the position of the people within the ship?" asked Roberts. "It would be hopeless to get them individually in the same positions. I've been trying to figure out the results both ways, but I can't see it."

"It wouldn't make any difference," said Mayhew-b. "Equation one twenty-three there shows that it's not the material elements of the ship in relationship to each other that matter but, rather, the position of the field that the entire structure represents. If that coincides with the other field, unity will result."

"I'm wondering what will happen to *us*," said Mayhew-a, glancing at his double.

"Why, there will continue to be two of us," said Mayhew-b. "Equation two forty-one here allows for the substitution of duplicates from other sets without reduction to unity. That's what will happen to us. Let's work it out in detail and see—"

He was suddenly interrupted by the hurried approach of Drangue. "Mayhew! Come quickly!" the Captain demanded. "Jeff Wicks has murdered Calvert Mason and escaped with Susan Dawning in one of the Rafts!"

Mayhew-b leaped up, his face blanched. "Come on! We'll follow in the other Raft. Drangue—take the *Express* out to C set and wait for us there!"

Roberts and Mayhew-a had difficulty in keeping up with Mayhew-b as he sped down the ramps and corridors of the ship towards the port where the remaining Raft lay.

"All of us had better go," said Mayhew-b. "We'll need all the brains available to track them down. That fool Wicks hasn't the slightest notion of what he's doing."

Mayhew-b took the controls; Mayhew-a and Roberts took up their places behind in the small control area.

"Swing through the sets of C," suggested Mayhew-a. "If Wicks started punching buttons at random that's probably where he's roaming right now. Our only hope is that the guide beam doesn't fade out."

"It shouldn't. It was built to be as permanent as that of the *Express*."

"Jeff might find a way to kill it."

"He doesn't know that much about it. The fool must have been drunk or crazy to run off into the sets that way."

"You can be sure he was drunk—but I can't figure out Susan. Why did she run off with him?"

Mayhew-b's lips were set. "Heaven only knows, but she had a reason. Yon can bank on that. I'd like to know where Jeff thinks he's going."

"I'd say that he doesn't," said Roberts. "Just panic flight reaction."

The others agreed, then fell silent while they watched the indicator as the counting of the N0 sets progressed. After a dozen counting cycles, Mayhew-b turned it off. "They aren't in an Aleph-Null set. You're probably right—he must have accidentally shifted to CC."

"Set it to count the C sets."

Mayhew-b rearranged the circuit configuration and resumed the operation of the counter circuits. They waited expectantly for the kick of the needle and the automatic indication of the set containing the Raft.

SLOWLY the knuckles of Mayhew-b's hand grew white as he clenched the end of the control desk. The counting cycle passed without an indication of the vagrant Raft. Another cycle began and ran its course.

"The thing couldn't have vanished completely," said Mayhew-b. "It's got to be in existence *somewhere.*"

"Look," said Mayhew-a, "do you remember exactly how the controls were set up on your Raft when you left it?"

"Sure, they were set to count and find the set of the *Express.* No, wait a minute, the counting circuit was off because you gave me the coordinates and I simply followed the guide beam in."

"All right. Suppose Jeff got in and took a hasty look at the panel and saw the Start button. He would push it. Where would that take him with the setup you had?"

"Why—to the *Express*. In that case, he wouldn't have moved anywhere."

"But he did move. Where could he have gone then?"

"The Raft must have jumped a couple of sets, but that seems impossible."

"Maybe not. The *Express* engines were idling, and for all we know they still contain the same defect that made the ship jump sets the first time. That might have caused the Raft to jump."

"Well, it's worth a try," said Mayhew-b. He reset the controls and returned the Raft to the side of the *Express* at the opposite port where the missing Raft had been.

He set up the board as it had been in his own Raft, then punched the Start button.

In that instant Mayhew-a knew he had been right. A terrible crushing force bore down upon each molecule of his being with intolerable destructiveness. It lasted for only a minute, then they were at the bottom of a sea of blood-red liquid. The scarlet hue burned into their eyes even through their lids and the vertigo of weightlessness sickened them.

Slowly the Raft seemed to be rising in that eternal world of sickening red. It rose and the liquid thinned until it was no more and the Raft was on a vast sphere whose horizons were an infinity away.

"Mayhew! There's Susan!" Roberts' sudden exclamation whirled them about to face the direction of his pointing finger. But they could see nothing but the bright alien sky beyond the horizon.

"What are you talking about?" demanded Mayhew-b.

"I saw her, I tell you. She was standing outside the Raft for just an instant pressing her face against the mesh, begging to get in. Then she was gone."

Mayhew-a felt a prickling cold wave traverse his spine. The higher the step in the hierarchy of the transfinite, the more ghostly it seemed. But it was impossible that Susan could have been out there. Life outside the Raft would be impossible.

"I tell you I saw her—"

Mayhew-b set the counter in operation again, with the necessary adjustments, and it had scarcely been turned on when the indicator swung over and held steady on the pin.

"We've got them!" he exclaimed.

Swiftly, he manipulated the controls to swing them into the same CC set as the other Raft. As he did so, the needle swung back towards zero on the indicator, but the Raft had been set in motion to arrive at the selected set. When it arrived they saw their quarry in the midst of that great plain on the surface of the sphere.

But that was not what held them speechless. Mayhew rose from his seat at the control panel and cried out, "Susan!"

The others pressed against the side of the cage.

For there upon that endless plain was Susan Dawning, but not Susan as they looked for her. As far as the eye could see there were infinite thousands of Susans running simultaneously in waves across the surface of that unknown world. And in the distance the Raft bearing Jeff Wicks was slowly vanishing from their sight—and from Susan's, for that was the goal of the running Susans.

There was something infinitely appalling about that expanse of Susans running with arms outflung towards the now vanished Raft. As the machine disappeared from sight, the figures stopped their mad flight and crumpled to the surface of the plain.

"How can it be?" gasped Roberts. "I don't see—"

"She's in a set below us," said Mayhew, "and somehow she's visible to us. We must be bridging the sets somehow. I wouldn't have thought it mathematically possible."

Then the Susans saw the second Raft and the endless millions rose and began running towards it.

"Carl!" The single word uttered from the Aleph number of throats produced a thunderous wave of sound.

"She can see us and we can see her," said Mayhew-b. "But how can we ever get to her? We can't possibly identify the set she's in even if we can see her, because there is no guide beam. I'm going out there with her."

Mayhew-a opened his mouth to speak, then shut it as his face distorted with indecision. Finally he said, "I don't see how she got out of the Raft or why she left Wicks—"

Mayhew-b slipped open the catch on the door opening outward, but a sudden change seemed to have taken place outside. The Susans were running in wild flight towards the Raft, but they seemed to be slipping farther and farther back on all sides as if they were running on a power treadmill that was carrying them backward.

Again that mighty, despairing cry rose from their throats. "Carl—help me!"

CHAPTER SEVEN
The Final Mystery

MAYHEW-b leaped out and ran towards them. The other two men dared not touch the controls of the Raft, yet they could see that the machine must be slipping from its unstable position on the borderline between the sets.

Mayhew-b grasped the hand of the nearest Susan and began dragging her towards the machine. In turn, she grasped her neighbor and a third was brought in tow before the chain was broken.

As if by the force of mighty will, Mayhew-b seemed to be making headway against the unknown currents drifting against him.

"Give a hand!" he called.

Roberts stepped out to the tenuous substance of the plain about them and extended a hand to the struggling figures. Slowly they edged back. At last they were close enough for Mayhew-a to reach out a hand while yet maintaining hold upon the Raft.

In a moment they were inside the cage and the door slammed shut. Almost simultaneously, the infinity of Susans vanished with a despairing wail. The plain became a barren waste of light and flowing, unknown forces of the transfinite.

No one spoke as Mayhew-a stepped to the controls to bring them back to the *Express*. In the crowded control area of the Raft, the men were silent. The three Susans sobbed quietly, looking from Mayhew-b to each other in desperation. Mayhew-b impulsively reached out a hand to comfort the nearest Susan and the pain that came into the eyes of the others overwhelmed him.

Incredibly, the three identical girls remained as the ship passed through the infinite sets and shifted transfinities on the return journey.

Abruptly, Mayhew-a uttered an exclamation as the Raft came out into a barren area. "Here's Tantalus. I thought the ship was still here, since we didn't detect it on the way down."

But apparently the *Tantalus Express* had left the Pleasure Planet to keep its rendezvous somewhere in C as the Mayhews had requested. Mayhew-a drove the ship back up to the higher set and adjusted the counter circuit.

"It would be like that trolley conductor to get lost again," muttered Roberts.

The men kept their eyes upon the indicator, while the now quiet Susans stared unbelievingly at their surroundings. "What were you doing in the Raft with Wicks?" Mayhew-b asked gently. "How did you ever get out here with him?"

The girls looked at each other, then one of them spoke hesitantly. "I was kidnapped. Jeff was drunk or crazy—or both. He said if he took me along no one would dare come after him because you—and I—"

"We won't have to worry about him anymore, I'm sure," said Mayhew-b. To wander aimlessly through eternity among the infinities would be suitable punishment for him, Mayhew-b thought. But what of the infinity of crying Susans lost in the eternal transfinite? Were they real? Did those cries of anguish he had heard have meaning? And what of the three whom had been snatched into reality by the motion of the Raft across the transfinite?

He felt his brain involuntarily closing the portals of thought to these questions to which there might never be answer. He doubted that the mathematics of the transfinite would develop enough in a hundred years to answer them.

And that would not help the pain in his heart as he thought of the anguished cries of the lost Susans—and the problems of the three beside him. Suddenly the nearest threw herself into his arms and cried, and his arms folded about her, his eyes closing to the presence of the other two.

He was brought back to the urgency of their present condition by the muttering of Mayhew-a. "Ten cycles and no indication of the *Express!*" the latter said. "The thing is just lost again, that's all."

Suddenly Roberts spoke up. "I'll bet I know what that trolley conductor did... When you were on Tantalus he said he was going back to Earth regardless of what you said. That's what he's done! We'll never find the ship now, because it's taken up a duplicate existence in some Aleph-Null set, and we have no means of finding it again."

Mayhew-a sagged back in the seat. The technician was undoubtedly right. Drangue, with his utter lack of imagination and knowledge of the transfinite, had carried out his threat and taken the ship to Earth.

At last he said, "Well, that leaves only us to worry about."

Mayhew-b turned to the three girls and said, "Back on Tantalus I promised you an explanation of what had happened. I'm going to give you that explanation now and try to help you understand all its implications. On Tantalus you saw an exact duplicate of yourself doing a broadcast of your show. And here you see two men, my brother and me, who are actually one and the same man.

"Don't ask me to explain how that can be. It's only explicable in mathematical terms that a dozen or so men in the world can fathom. But just as Carl Mayhew has become more than one, so, likewise have you. And so has everyone aboard the *Tantalus Express*. It's a problem that no one has ever faced before. We thought we had an answer that would enable us to return to Earth as one instead of having duplicates there. But that involved machinery aboard the *Express* which we do not have on this little ship. Therefore, we've got to go back. Once there, perhaps we can do something about it, but for now we've got to bare the fact of this multiple existence. Of all the people aboard the *Express*, you were the sanest in time of crisis, Susan. I'm depending on you to maintain that sanity now."

The girls nodded slowly, but in the eyes of each was the terrible question that lay heavily upon Mayhew-b. He had meant to ask Susan Dawning to be his wile. *But which of these—?*

Mayhew-a said suddenly, "There may still be one chance. Drangue may not have done as we suspected. He may have slipped into a higher system as before. We may as well look as far as we can go."

Roberts and Mayhew-b nodded, though they had little faith in their chances of finding the *Express*. They knew Drangue and his kind. He had been scared stiff through the whole experience. A final panic reaction had driven him to the nearest haven.

Mayhew-a advanced the ship into C° and let the counter circuits run through a dozen cycles. The result was completely negative.

"We may as well go to Earth," said Roberts.

"We hit a higher set once. I'm going to try it again."

He made some adjustments behind the panel, then sat down again and threw the power on. Abruptly, agonies of nausea seized them and they were at the bottom of the sea of blood as they entered the realm above C°.

Mayhew-a half expected, half hoped to see the endless expanse of crying Susans again, but he knew it was vain. There was utterly no chance of striking the same set where those figures had been encountered.

But Mayhew-b and Roberts were staring at the indicator and shouting in spite of their sickness. "We've got it. There's an indication of the *Express!*"

They came to rest in the midst of that barren plain after rising through the sea of blood. And there in the infinite distances of this realm lay the *Express*.

With satisfaction that his guess had been right, Mayhew-a stepped the acceleration of the Raft up to the maximum and slowly the *Express* grew as their terrific velocity brought them closer.

Roberts exclaimed. "Look! Jeff Wicks must be back—there's a Raft by the ship."

Mayhew-b verified the fact. "I wonder how in the world he ever found it. Certainly he knows nothing of guiding the Raft, yet an accident of that kind is impossible."

"We probably won't have anything to worry about from him," said Mayhew-b. "I imagine he's in custody by now. Drangue would have sense enough for that, at least."

There was no sign of activity aboard the ship as the Raft approached. It drew up slowly and merged its field with that of the *Express* against a closed port of the larger vessel. Then Mayhew-a opened the communicator circuits. "Drangue, this is the Raft. Mayhew talking. Open up."

In a moment, the screen in the Raft lighted and Drangue's florid face appeared. He stared and then his eyes went wide, and a hoarse exclamation came from his throat. "Mayhew!"

Mayhew-a growled in disgust. "What's the matter with him, anyway?"

Then Mayhew-b grabbed his arm and pointed toward the screen. "Look!"

There, staring in unbelief, was an image of themselves.

"Roberts was right," said Mayhew-a slowly. "We've found the wrong ship. This isn't the one we were aboard before."

ADMITTED at last to the control room, they sat down and tried to comprehend this new situation. Mayhew-a addressed the new Mayhew. "I'm 'a'," he said, "and this is 'b'. For purposes of reference you may as well be 'c'."

"Suits me, but how many are there of us, anyway?"

"We'll never know, I'm beginning to think." Rapidly then, Mayhew, brought him up to date on their experiences. "What I'd like to know," he finished, "is where you and I separated. Did we originate in the same set and split later, or did we start out from altogether different Aleph Nulls?"

"We started out together, quite obviously," said Mayhew-c. "We split when the Raft found a guide beam leading to the *Express*. The *Express* itself exploded into a thousand sets. My—our—Raft responded to at least two, and possibly more. You went after one and I went after the other."

At that moment the door opened and a woman entered. Mayhew-b rose with a start. His face blanched. The newcomer was Susan Dawning. She saw him first and came towards him with a smile.

Then Mayhew-c said, "Just a moment, dear. These gentlemen are—ah—visitors."

The girl turned and gasped, her eyes glancing back and forth between the three duplicate men, and then at the three girls who were images of herself.

"Gentlemen, allow me to present my wife. We were married two days ago by Captain Drangue."

After the initial moments of confusion and surprise had worn off, they seated themselves about the table in the control room, three Mayhews, four Susans, and two Robertses.

"Out problem has not changed," Mayhew-a began slowly, "despite the fact that the *Express* we were previously aboard has gone back to Earth in a set where its occupants will be duplicates. Nor despite the fact that there may yet be other ships like this wandering through the *interim* beyond our reach.

"Reality, for us, is that which can be perceived by our senses or brought into range of perception by mechanical means. We know that the multiple perceptions of C will reduce to unity in Aleph-Null. The elements that have become unique: the other *Express* we know of, and those that may yet be lost; the images of Susan; Jeff Wicks—all of these must be considered to have no reality with respect to us when we return to Earth. It is the only way to keep our sanity, to consider it in this way."

He turned to Mayhew-c. "Our Roberts did some mathematical work that indicated an almost positive return to Aleph-Null in a unity condition. It involved the time mechanism of the *Express*. What work have you done?"

Mayhew-c answered, "Our Roberts did similar work. We have nearly completed the adjusting and testing of the time circuits. It appears that even though we have lost congruency, there remains some similarity."

"How long have you been here?"

"About six weeks."

"There's a time difference. How did you keep the passengers from rioting?"

"Finally drugged them through the air system. We'll have to give them the antidote right away because we can make a trial return within an hour."

"The problem of the *Express* and its passengers in the set to which we return will be solved," said Mayhew-b. "I am confident of that, but for those of us in this room it will not be solved."

"Susan and I already have our answer for that," said Mayhew-c. "We decided even before you came that we would not go back."

"What do you intend to do?"

"Well, I've always had a hankering to quit Trans-Astra and get into research and consulting work—as you well know, of course. Susan is really just a bit tired of show life, so what would be easier than to just let the ship return without us? Our duplicates will be there to carry our work on and we will be free to do as we wish. We intend to take the Raft to Tantalus for a two-week honeymoon, then we'll probably come to Earth and start our new lives under some other names."

Mayhew-b nodded miserably. "That's a nice plan, so simple and easy, but for me—"

One of the Susans put a hand on his arm. "I know what you're thinking, Carl. It will all work out in the end. I know it will. I've heard something of what has been discussed concerning change of experience producing change of individuals. It's obvious in you three Mayhews. We'll all go to Earth and take up individual existences. In a year's time there won't be three Susans for you to worry about—there may not even be one."

"Susan!"

"I'm beginning to think my first estimate was wrong," said Mayhew-a.

Mayhew-b brightened. "Then maybe you—"

"Oh, no," Mayhew-a replied in quick embarrassment. "Strictly the bachelor type—strictly."

The conference broke up. The wife of Mayhew-c invited the three other Susans to come with her while work was resumed on the time mechanism of the *Tantalus Express*. Drangue was ordered to administer an antidote for the drugs used to subdue the many stupefied passengers who were moving slowly about the ship like mechanical men or zombies.

Mayhew-c's estimate of the time required to finish the work had been generous. With all of them lending a hand, it was completed and finally tested within a half-hour.

Mayhew-c stood up and surveyed the intricate mechanism. "Well—that's that," There was an awkward pause as the duplicate Mayhews looked at each other. "I guess Susan and I had better get off so you can get on back where you belong," said Mayhew-c.

From the ports of the control room the others watched Mayhew-c and his wife enter the Raft. They could be seen through the mesh roof, waving a gay goodbye, and then suddenly they vanished, swallowed up by the transfinite.

"It gives me the willies," said Roberts, shuddering. "If I ever hear anybody mention the word transfinite after we get back I'll punch him one."

"Want to bet?" said Mayhew-a. "You'll be back on your old job at Trans-Astra within a week."

"Which one of us?" said the other Roberts.

"You could trade off. A week's work—a week's fishing. It would have advantages."

"We're all ready," said Mayhew-b abruptly.

Despite their confidence, there was a moment's hesitation as they faced the test of getting the *Express* back to its own set so that it would combine in unity relationship with the *Express* from Tantalus.

"Shall we get the Susans up here?" said Mayhew-a.

"No—no, we may as well go as we are. We'll know in a moment if we're successful."

He threw the switches.

THE GLARE of light in the landing area bathed the body of the *Tantalus Express* in a sea of light. Like some ghostly vision out of another world, the ship solidified before the eyes of the hundreds of spectators, newsmen, and photographers, who were waiting to greet those aboard the gigantic ship.

It was always a great thing to see the *Express* come in. It would never become a commonplace, the sudden appearance of this monster machine from seventeen thousand light years away.

From the control room Mayhew watched the milling crowds and heard the gangplank rumble as they reached out in a score of places to permit the disembarkation of the many passengers.

They had made it, Mayhew thought. He submerged in his mind the dim questions of what was reality. *This* was reality, this Aleph-Null set in which he existed. There were no other Earths, no other ships like the *Tantalus Express*. This was reality. There was not even any other—

Mayhew!

His brain closed itself against thought under the impact of sudden realization. That Equation 241 that he had been going to follow up just before they left Tantalus—it had given him only the wraith of an idea of what would happen.

He was Mayhew. In his brain were the double memory patterns of Mayhew-a and Mayhew-b who had reduced to unity in the Aleph-Null set.

And Roberts was standing there, a single Roberts. "I guess we don't have to worry about being double, after all. Someday I'm going to find out what goes on in the transfinite—"

But Mayhew wasn't listening. He rushed from the control room. Out on the mezzanine he could see the streams of departing passengers. Most of them would put it down as a bad dream, he thought. Lucky that they had been in a state of stupefaction during most of the time in the *interim*.

Suddenly he glimpsed two familiar figures, Calvert Mason, and his nephew, Jeff Wicks.

Should he warn Mason, he thought? But wasn't there in Mason's brain the memory pattern of being killed? No—that had been the other Mason, the one Drangue took to Earth.

Perhaps Jeff would not attempt to kill Mason as he had done in that unique set created by the appearance of the *Express* on its unexpected and unauthorized trip to Tantalus.

But nothing *he* could say or do would alter the course of events, he realized. He wished momentarily he had taken the course Mayhew-c had followed. He hadn't realized the full extent of the difference between Mayhew-a and Mayhew-b. His powers of adjustment would be strained to the breaking point until the conflicting viewpoints were reconciled or one of them became dominant.

He heard the sudden sound of running feet and turned to face Susan.

"Carl! Carl!" She ran towards him with outstretched arms and buried her face against his chest. "I'm so mixed up in my mind. Oh, tell me what it's all about, Carl."

She would be as confused as he was, he thought. More so, because she lacked his understanding of events. And within her brain was the memory pattern of the Susan who had come direct from Tantalus to Earth, the Susan who had fallen in love with Mayhew-b, and the trio of Susans who had been rescued from among the horde in the *interim*—

"It's going to be all right," said Mayhew softly. "I'll help you understand it all and it'll straighten itself out."

The consulting business was a good idea, he thought. Mayhew-c would probably not appear in this set, so they would not run into each other. And there was still a Mayhew employed by Trans-Astra who was sleeping in his apartment, totally ignorant of all these weird and incredible happenings.

Mayhew suddenly drew Susan close and held her tightly in his arms. "It'll take time, but I'll help you understand those memories in your mind, and some of them will fade until they are only bad dreams."

For himself, his problem was solved, he thought abruptly. Mayhew-b was going to dominate, by a long shot.

THE END

If you've enjoyed this book, you will not want to miss these terrific titles…

ARMCHAIR SCI-FI & HORROR DOUBLE NOVELS, $12.95 each

D-31 **A HOAX IN TIME** by Keith Laumer
INSIDE EARTH by Poul Anderson

D-32 **TERROR STATION** by Dwight V. Swain
THE WEAPON FROM ETERNITY by Dwight V. Swain

D-33 **THE SHIP FROM INFINITY** by Edmond Hamilton
TAKEOFF by C. M. Kornbluth

D-34 **THE METAL DOOM** by David H. Keller
TWELVE TIMES ZERO by Howard Browne

D-35 **HUNTERS OUT OF SPACE** by Joseph Kelleam
INVASION FROM THE DEEP by Paul W. Fairman,

D-36 **THE BEES OF DEATH** by Robert Moore Williams
A PLAGUE OF PYTHONS by Frederik Pohl

D-37 **THE LORDS OF QUARMALL** by Fritz Leiber and Harry Fischer
BEACON TO ELSEWHERE by James H. Schmitz

D-38 **BEYOND PLUTO** by John S. Campbell
ARTERY OF FIRE by Thomas N. Scortia

D-39 **SPECIAL DELIVERY** by Kris Neville
NO TIME FOR TOFFEE by Charles F. Meyers

D-40 **JUNGLE IN THE SKY** by Milton Lesser
RECALLED TO LIFE by Robert Silverberg

ARMCHAIR SCIENCE FICTION CLASSICS, $12.95 each

C-10 **MARS IS MY DESTINATION**
by Frank Belknap Long

C-11 **SPACE PLAGUE**
by George O. Smith

C-12 **SO SHALL YE REAP**
by Rog Phillips

ARMCHAIR SCI-FI & HORROR GEMS SERIES, $12.95 each

G-3 **SCIENCE FICTION GEMS, Vol. Two**
James Blish and others

G-4 **HORROR GEMS, Vol. Two**
Joseph Payne Brennan and others

If you've enjoyed this book, you will not want to miss these terrific titles...

ARMCHAIR SCI-FI & HORROR DOUBLE NOVELS, $12.95 each

D -41   **FULL CYCLE** by Clifford D. Simak
        IT WAS THE DAY OF THE ROBOT by Frank Belknap Long

D-42   **THIS CROWDED EARTH** by Robert Bloch
        REIGN OF THE TELEPUPPETS by Daniel Galouye

D-43   **THE CRISPIN AFFAIR** by Jack Sharkey
        THE RED HELL OF JUPITER by Paul Ernst

D-44   **PLANET OF DREAD** by Dwight V. Swain
        WE THE MACHINE by Gerald Vance

D-45   **THE STAR HUNTER** by Edmond Hamilton
        THE ALIEN by Raymond F. Jones

D-46   **WORLD OF IF** by Rog Phillips
        SLAVE RAIDERS FROM MERCURY by Don Wilcox

D-47   **THE ULTIMATE PERIL** by Robert Abernathy
        PLANET OF SHAME by Bruce Elliot

D-48   **THE FLYING EYES** by J. Hunter Holly
        SOME FABULOUS YONDER by Phillip Jose Farmer

D-49   **THE COSMIC BUNGLERS** by Geoff St. Reynard
        THE BUTTONED SKY by Geoff St. Reynard

D-50   **TYRANTS OF TIME** by Milton Lesser
        PARIAH PLANET by Murray Leinster

ARMCHAIR SCIENCE FICTION CLASSICS, $12.95 each

C-13   **SUNKEN WORLD**
        by Stanton A. Coblentz

C-14   **THE LAST VIAL**
        by Sam McClatchie, M. D.

C-15   **WE WHO SURVIVED (THE FIFTH ICE AGE)**
        by Sterling Noel

ARMCHAIR MASTERS OF SCIENCE FICTION SERIES, $16.95 each

MS-5   **MASTERS OF SCIENCE FICTION, Vol. Five**
        Winston K. Marks—Test Colony and other tales

MS-6   **MASTERS OF SCIENCE FICTION, Vol. Six**
        Fritz Leiber—Deadly Moon and other tales

If you've enjoyed this book, you will not want to miss these terrific titles…

ARMCHAIR SCI-FI & HORROR DOUBLE NOVELS, $12.95 each

D -91 **THE TIME TRAP** by Henry Kuttner
THE LUNAR LICHEN by Hal Clement

D-92 **SARGASSO OF LOST STARSHIPS** by Poul Anderson
THE ICE QUEEN by Don Wilcox

D-93 **THE PRINCE OF SPACE** by Jack Williamson
POWER by Harl Vincent

D-94 **PLANET OF NO RETURN** by Howard Browne
THE ANNIHILATOR COMES by Ed Earl Repp

D-95 **THE SINISTER INVASION** by Edmond Hamilton
OPERATION TERROR by Murray Leinster

D-96 **TRANSIENT** by Ward Moore
THE WORLD-MOVER by George O. Smith

D-97 **FORTY DAYS HAS SEPTEMBER** by Milton Lesser
THE DEVIL'S PLANET by David Wright O'Brien

D-98 **THE CYBERENE** by Rog Phillips
BADGE OF INFAMY by Lester del Rey

D-99 **THE JUSTICE OF MARTIN BRAND** by Raymond A. Palmer
BRING BACK MY BRAIN by Dwight V. Swain

D-100 **WIDE-OPEN PLANET** by L. Sprague de Camp
AND THEN THE TOWN TOOK OFF by Richard Wilson

ARMCHAIR SCIENCE FICTION CLASSICS, $12.95 each

C-31 **THE GOLDEN GUARDSMEN**
by S. J. Byrne

C-32 **ONE AGAINST THE MOON**
by Donald A. Wollheim

C-33 **HIDDEN CITY**
by Chester S. Geier

ARMCHAIR SCI-FI & HORROR GEMS SERIES, $12.95 each

G-9 **SCIENCE FICTION GEMS, Vol. Five**
Clifford D. Simak and others

G-10 **HORROR GEMS, Vol. Five**
E. Hoffman Price and others

If you've enjoyed this book, you will not want to miss these terrific titles…

ARMCHAIR SCI-FI & HORROR DOUBLE NOVELS, $12.95 each

D -111   **THE MOON ERA** by Jack Williamson
REVENGE OF THE ROBOTS by Howard Browne

D-112   **SON OF THE BLACK CHALICE** by Milton Lesser
SENTRY OF THE SKY by Evelyn E. Smith

D-113   **OUTPOST ON THE MOON** by Joslyn Maxwell
POTENTIAL ZERO by S. J. Byrne

D-114   **OUTPOST INFINITY** by Raymond F. Jones
THE WHITE INVADERS by Ray Cummings

D-115   **TIME TRAP** by Rog Phillips
THE COSMIC DESTROYER by Alexander Blade

D-116   **THE OTHER SIDE OF THE MOON** by Edmond Hamilton
SECRET INVASION by Walter Kubilius

D-117   **DANGER MOON** by Frederik Pohl
THE HIDDEN UNIVERSE by Ralph Milne Farley

D-118   **THE WAILING ASTEROID** by Murray Leinster
THE WORLD THAT COULDN'T BE by Clifford D. Simak

D-119   **THE WHISPERING GORILLA** by Don Wilcox
RETURN OF THE WHISPERING GORILLA by David V. Reed

D-120   **SPECIAL EFFECT** by J. F. Bone
WARLORD OF KOR by Terry Carr

ARMCHAIR SCIENCE FICTION CLASSICS, $12.95 each

C-37   **THE GREEN MAN RETURNS**
by Harold M. Sherman

C-38   **THE SHAVER MYSTERY, Book Five**
by Richard S, Shaver

C-39   **MARS CHILD**
by Cyril Judd

ARMCHAIR MASTERS OF SCIENCE FICTION SERIES, $16.95 each

MS-9   **MASTERS OF SCIENCE FICTION AND FANTASY, Vol. Nine**
Poul Anderson, "The Star Beast" and other tales

MS-10   **MASTERS OF SCIENCE FICTION, Vol. Ten**
Robert Moore Williams, "Time Tolls for Toro" and other tales

A DEADLY THREAT FROM THE FOURTH DIMENSION

When a young boy told Don Livingston that he'd seen what he thought was a ghost, Don could only chuckle at the young man, to whom he gave assurances that ghosts were far from real. However, to prove the boy wrong, and perhaps even out of a strangely compelling sense of curiosity, Livingston and one of his pals checked out the distant hill where the boy had seen his apparition. The boy had described it as "a ghost that had floated toward him and passed through a rock." Livingston, with shotgun in hand, soon discovered he wasn't dealing with a ghost. Nor was it a wild animal. Much to his amazement Don Livingston discovered that he was facing the very real threat of an invasion from another realm—the fourth dimension.

They came to be known as "the White Invaders," and every human on Earth was faced with extermination if they weren't stopped!

ABOUT RAY CUMMINGS...

Born in New York City in 1887, sci-fi great Ray Cummings' writings showed great insight into the vast possibilities of future science. Much of this grew out of Cummings' personal relationship with American genius, Thomas Alva Edison.

During the 1920's and 1930's Cummings mesmerized thousands of readers with his amazing tales of time, other dimensions, and outer space. Tales like *Girl in the Golden Atom*, *Brigands of the Moon*, and *Wandl the Invader* established Cummings as a genre writer of the first magnitude. His imagination supplied a great many of the most basic motifs that current science fiction holds dear, even to this day. While he followed in the tradition of other greats like Jules Verne and H. G. Wells, he also bridged the gap between those early masters and a newer style of sci-fi and fantasy writing that exploded into the field in the early and middle decades of the Twentieth Century.

When Ray Cummings passed away in January of 1957, the world of modern science fiction lost one of its true founding fathers.

THE WHITE INVADERS

By
RAY CUMMINGS

ARMCHAIR FICTION
PO Box 4369, Medford, Oregon   97501-0168

*For more information about Armchair Books and products, visit our
website at…*

www.armchairfiction.com

Or email us at…

armchairfiction@yahoo.com

CHAPTER ONE
A White Shape in the Moonlight

THE colored boy gazed at Don and me with a look of terror.

"But I tell you I seen it!" he insisted. "An' it's down there now. A ghost! It's all white an' shinin'!"

"Nonsense, Willie," Don turned to me. "I say, Bob, what do you make of this?"

"I seen it, I tell you," the boy broke in. "It ain't a mile from here if you want to go look at it."

Don gripped the colored boy whose coffee complexion had taken on a greenish cast with his terror.

I fired at an oncoming white figure.

"Stop saying that, Willie. That's absolute rot. There's no such thing as a ghost."

"But I seen—"

"Where?"

"Over on the north shore. Not far."

"What did you see?" Don shook him. "Tell us exactly."

"A man! I seen a man. He was up on a cliff just by the golf course when I first seen him. I was comin' along the path down by the Fort Beach an' I looked up an' there he was, shinin' all white in the moonlight. An' then before I could run, he came floatin' down at me."

"Floating?"

"Yes. He didn't walk. He came down through the rocks. I could see the rocks of the cliff right through him."

Don laughed at that. But neither he nor I could set this down as utter nonsense, for within the past week there had been many wild stories of ghosts among the colored people of Bermuda. The Negroes of Bermuda are not unduly superstitious, and certainly they are more intelligent, better educated than most of their race. But the little islands, this past week, were echoing with whispered tales of strange things seen at night. It had been mostly down at the lower end of the comparatively inaccessible Somerset; but now here it was in our own neighborhood.

"You've got the fever, Willie," Don laughed. "I say, who told you you saw a man walking through rock?"

"Nobody told me. I seen him. It ain't far if you—"

"You think he's still there?"

"Maybe so. Mr. Don, he was standin' still, with his arms folded. I ran, an'—"

"Let's go see if he's there," I suggested. "I'd like to have a look at one of these ghosts."

BUT even as I lightly said it, a queer thrill of fear shot through me. No one can contemplate an encounter with the supernatural without a shudder.

"Right you are," Don exclaimed. "What's the use of theory? Can you lead us to where you saw him, Willie?"

"Ye-es, of course."

The sixteen-year-old Willie was shaking again. "W-what's that for, Mr. Don?"

Don had picked up a shotgun which was standing in a corner of the room.

"Ain't no—no use of that, Mr. Don."

"We'll take it anyway, Willie. Ready, Bob?"

A step sounded behind us. "Where are you going?"

It was Jane Dorrance, Don's cousin. She stood in the doorway. Her long, filmy white summer dress fell nearly to her ankles. Her black hair was coiled on her head. In her bodice was a single red poinsettia blossom. As she stood motionless, her small slight figure framed against the dark background of the hall, she could have been a painting of an English beauty save for the black hair suggesting the tropics. Her blue-eyed gaze went from Don to me, and then to the gun.

"Where are you going?"

"Willie saw a ghost." Don grinned. "They've come from Somerset, Jane. I say, one of them seems to be right here."

"Where?"

"Willie saw it down by the Fort Beach."

"To-night?"

"Yes. Just now. So he says, though it's all rot, of course."

"Oh," said Jane, and she became silent.

SHE appeared to be barring our way. It seemed to me, too, that the color had left her face, and I wondered vaguely why she was taking it so seriously. That was not like Jane: she was a level-headed girl, not at all the sort to be frightened by Negroes talking of ghosts.

She turned suddenly on Willie. The colored boy had been employed in the Dorrance household since childhood. Jane herself was only seventeen, and she had known Willie here in this same big white stone house, almost from infancy.

"Willie, what you saw, was it a—a man?"

"Yes," said the boy eagerly. "A man. A great big man. All white an' shinin'."

"A man with a hood? Or a helmet? Something like a queer-looking hat on his head, Willie?"

"Jane!" expostulated Don. "What do you mean?"

"I saw him—saw it," said Jane nervously.

"Good Lord!" I exclaimed. "You did? When? Why didn't you tell us?"

"I saw it last night." She smiled faintly. "I didn't want to add to these wild tales. I thought it was my imagination. I had been asleep—I fancy I was dreaming of ghosts anyway."

"You saw it—" Don prompted.

"Outside my bedroom window. Some time in the middle of the night. The moon was out and the—the man was all white and shining, just as Willie says."

"But your bedroom," I protested. "Good Lord, your bedroom is on the upper floor."

But Jane continued soberly, with a sudden queer hush to her voice, "It was standing in the air outside my window. I think it had been looking in. When I sat up—I think I had cried out, though none of you heard me evidently—when I sat up, it moved away; walked away. When I got to the window, there was nothing to see." She smiled again. "I decided it was all part of my dream. This morning—well, I was afraid to tell you because I knew you'd laugh at me. So many girls down in Somerset have been imagining things like that."

TO me, this was certainly a new light on the matter. I think that both Don and I, and certainly the police, had vaguely been of the opinion that some very human trickster was at the bottom of all this. Someone, criminal or otherwise, against whom our shotgun would be efficacious. But here was level-headed Jane telling us of a man standing in mid-air peering into her second-floor bedroom, and then walking away. No trickster could accomplish that.

"Ain't we goin'?" Willie demanded. "I seen it, but it'll be gone."

"Right enough," Don exclaimed grimly. "Come on, Willie."

He disregarded Jane as he walked to the door, but she clung to him.

"I'm coming," she said obstinately, and snatched a white lace scarf from the hall rack and flung it over her head like a mantilla. "Don, may I come?" she added coaxingly.

He gazed at me dubiously. "Why, I suppose so," he said finally. Then he grinned. "Certainly no harm is going to come to us from a ghost. Might frighten us to death, but that's about all a ghost can do, isn't it?"

We left the house. The only other member of the Dorrance household was Jane's father—the Hon. Arthur Dorrance, M.P. He had been in Hamilton all day, and had not yet returned. It was about nine o'clock of an evening in mid-May. The huge moon rode high in a fleecy sky, illumining the island with a light so bright one could almost read by it.

"We'll walk," said Don. "No use riding, Willie."

"No. It's shorter over the hill. It ain't far."

WE left our bicycles standing against the front veranda, and, with Willie and Don leading us, we plunged off along the little dirt road of the Dorrance estate. The poinsettia blooms were thick on both sides of us. A lily field, which a month before had been solid white with blossoms, still added its redolence to the perfumed night air. Through the branches of the squat cedar trees, in almost every direction there was water visible—deep purple this night, with a rippled sheen of silver upon it.

We reached the main road, a twisting white ribbon in the moonlight. We followed it for a little distance, around a corkscrew turn, across a tiny causeway where the moonlit water of an inlet lapped against the base of the road and the sea-breeze fanned us. A carriage, heading into the nearby town of St. Georges, passed us with the thud of horses' hoofs pounding on the hard smooth stone of the road. Under its jaunty canopy an American man reclined with a girl on each side of him. He waved us a jovial greeting as they passed.

Then Willie turned us off the road. We climbed the ramp of an open grassy field, with a little cedar woods to one side, and up ahead, half a mile to the right, the dark crumbling ramparts of a little ancient fort which once was for the defense of the island.

Jane and I were together, with Willie and Don in advance of us, and Don carrying the shotgun.

"You really saw it, Jane?"

"Oh, I don't know. I thought I did. Then I thought that I didn't."

"Well, I hope we see it now. And if it's human—which it must be if there's anything to it at all—we'll march it back to St. Georges and lock it up."

She turned and smiled at me, but it was a queer smile, and I must admit my own feelings were queer.

"Don't you think you're talking nonsense, Bob?"

"Yes, I do," I admitted. "I guess maybe the whole thing is nonsense. But it's got the police quite worried. You knew that, didn't you? All this wild talk—there must be some basis for it."

Don was saying, "Take the lower path, Willie. Take the same route you were taking when you saw it."

WE climbed down a steep declivity, shadowed by cedar trees, and reached the edge of a tiny, almost landlocked, lagoon. It was no more than a few hundred feet in diameter. The jagged, porous gray-black rocks rose like an upstanding crater rim to mark its ten-foot entrance to the sea. A little white house stood here with its back against the fifty-foot cliff. It was dark, its colored occupants probably already asleep. Two rowboats floated in the lagoon, moored near the shore. And on the narrow strip of stony beach, nets were spread to dry.

"This way, Mister Don. I was comin' along here, toward the Fort." Willie was again shaking with excitement. "Just past that bend."

"You keep behind me." Don led us now, with his gun half raised. "Don't talk when we get further along, and walk as quietly as you can."

The narrow path followed the bottom of the cliff. We presently had the open sea before us, with a line of reefs a few hundred yards out against which the lazy ground swell was breaking in a line of white. The moonlit water lapped gently at our feet. The cliff rose to our right, a mass of gray-black rock, pitted and broken, fantastically indented, unreal in the moonlight.

"I seen it—just about there," Willie whispered.

Before us, a little rock headland jutted out into the water. Don halted us, and we stood silent, gazing. I think that there is hardly any place more fantastic than a Bermuda shorefront in the moonlight. In these little eroded recesses, caves and grottoes one might expect to see crooked-legged gnomes, scampering to peer at the human intruder. Gnarled cedars, hanging precariously, might hide pixies and elves. A child's dream of fairyland, this reality of a Bermuda shorefront.

"There it is!"

WILLIE'S sibilant whisper dispelled my roaming fancy. We all turned to stare behind us in the direction of Willie's unsteady finger. And we all saw it—the white shape of a man down near the winding path we had just traversed. A wild thrill of fear, excitement, revulsion—call it what you will—surged over me. The thing had been following us!

We stood frozen, transfixed. The shape was almost at the water level, a hundred feet or so away. It had stopped its advance; to all appearances it was a man standing there, calmly regarding us. Don and I swung around to face it, shoving Jane and Willie behind us.

Willie had started off in terror, but Jane gripped him.

"Quiet, Willie!"

"There it is! See it—"

"Of course we see it," Don whispered. "Don't talk. We'll wait; see what it does."

We stood a moment. The thing was motionless. It was in a patch of shadow, but, as though gleaming with moonlight, it seemed to shine. Its glow was silvery, with a greenish cast almost phosphorescent. Was it standing on the path? I could not tell. It was too far away; too much in shadow. But I plainly saw that it had the shape of a man. Wraith, or substance? That also, was not yet apparent.

Then suddenly it was moving! Coming toward us. But not floating, for I could see the legs moving, the arms swaying. With measured tread it was walking slowly toward us!

Don's shotgun went up. "Bob, we'll hold our ground. Is it—is he armed, can you see?"

"No! Can't tell."

Armed! What nonsense! How could this wraith, this apparition, do us physical injury!

"If—if he gets too close, Bob, by God, I'll shoot. But if he's human, I wouldn't want to kill him."

THE shape had stopped again. It was fifty feet from us now, and we could clearly see that it was a man, taller than normal. He stood now with folded arms—a man strangely garbed in what seemed a white, tight-fitting jacket and short trunks. On his head was a black skull cap surmounted by a helmet of strange design.

Don's voice suddenly echoed across the rocks.

"Who are you?"

The white figure gave no answer. It did not move.

"We see you. What do you want?" Don repeated.

Then it moved again. Partly toward us and partly sidewise, away from the sea. The swing of the legs was obvious. It was walking. But not upon the path, nor upon the solid surface of these Bermuda rocks! A surge of horror went through me at the realization. This was nothing human! It was walking on some other surface, invisible to us, but something solid beneath its own tread.

"Look!" Jane whispered. "It's walking—*into the cliff!*"

There was no doubt about it now. Within thirty feet of us, it was slowly walking up what must have been a steep ascent. Already it was ten feet or more above our level. And it was behind the rocks of the cliff! Shining in there as though the rocks themselves were transparent!

Or were my senses tricking me? I whispered, "Is it back of the rocks? Or is there a cave over there? An opening?"

"Let's go see." Don took a step forward; and called again:

"You—we see you. Stand still! Do you want me to fire at you?"

The figure turned and again stood regarding us with folded arms. Obviously not Don's voice, but his movement, had stopped it. We left the path and climbed about ten feet up the broken cliff-side. The figure was at our level now, but it was within the rocks. We were close enough now to see other details: a man's white face, with heavy black brows, heavy features; a stalwart, giant figure, six and a half feet at the least. The white garment could have been of woven metal. I saw black, thread-like wires looped along the arms, over the shoulders, down the sides of the muscular naked legs. There seemed, at the waist, a dial-face, with wires running into it.

The details were so clear that they seemed substantial, real. Yet the figure was so devoid of color that it could have been a light-image projected here upon these rocks. And the contour of the cliff was plainly visible in front of it.

WE stood gazing at the thing, and it stared back at us.

"Can you hear us?" Don called.

Evidently it could not. Then a sardonic smile spread over the face of the apparition. The lips moved. It said something to us, but we heard no sound.

It was a wraith—this thing so visibly real! It was apparently close to us, yet there was a limitless, intervening void of the unknown.

It stood still with folded arms across the brawny chest, sardonically regarding us. The face was strangely featured, yet wholly of human cast. And, above all, its aspect was strangely evil. Its gaze suddenly turned on Jane with a look that made my heart leap into my throat and made me fling up my arms as though to protect her.

Then seemingly it had contemplated us enough; the folded arms swung down; it turned away from us, slowly stalking off.

"Stop!" Don called.

"See!" I whispered. "It's coming out in the open!"

The invisible surface upon which it walked led it out from the cliff. The figure was stalking away from us in mid-air, and it seemed to fade slowly in the moonlight.

"It's going!" I exclaimed. "Don, it's getting away!"

Impulsively I started scrambling over the rocks; unreasoningly, for who can chase and capture a ghost?

Don stopped me. "Wait!" His shotgun went to his shoulders. The white shape was now again about fifty feet away. The gun blazed into the moonlight. The buckshot tore through the stalking white figure; the moonlit shorefront echoed with the shot.

When the smoke cleared away, we saw the apparition still walking quietly forward. Up over the sea now, up and out into the moonlit night, growing smaller and dimmer in the distance, until presently it was faded and gone.

A ghost?

We thought so then.

CHAPTER TWO
The Face at the Window

THIS was our first encounter with the white invaders. It was too real to ignore or treat lightly. One may hear tales of a ghost, even the recounting by a most reliable eye-witness, and smile skeptically. But to see one yourself—as we had seen this thing in the moonlight of that Bermuda shorefront—that is a far different matter.

We told our adventure to Jane's father when he drove in from Hamilton about eleven o'clock that same evening. But he, who personally had seen no ghost, could only look perturbed that we should be so deluded. Some trickster— or some trick of the moonlight, and the shadowed rocks aiding our own sharpened imaginations. He could think of no other explanation. But Don had fired pointblank into the thing and had not harmed it.

Arthur Dorrance, member of the Bermuda Parliament, was a gray-haired gentleman in his fifties, a typical British Colonial, the present head of this old Bermuda family. The tales or the ghosts, whatever their origin, already had forced themselves upon Governmental attention. All this evening, in Hamilton, Mr. Dorrance had been in conference trying to determine what to do about it. Tales of terror in little Bermuda had a bad enough local effect, but to have them spread abroad, to influence adversely the tourist trade upon which Bermuda's very existence depended—that presaged economic catastrophe.

"And the tales are spreading," he told us. "Look here, you young cubs, it's horribly disconcerting to have you of all people telling me a thing like this."

Even now he could not believe us. But he sat staring at us, eyeglasses in hand, with his untouched drink before him.

"We'll have to report it, of course. I've been all evening with the steamship officials. They're having cancellations." He smiled faintly at me. "We can't get along without you Americans, Bob."

I have not mentioned that I am an American. I was on vacation from my job as radio technician in New York. Don Livingston, who is English and three years my senior, was in a similar line of work—at this time he was technician in the small Bermuda broadcasting station located in the nearby town of St. Georges.

WE talked until nearly midnight. Then the telephone rang. It was the Police Chief in Hamilton. Ghosts had been seen in that vicinity this evening. There were a dozen complaints of ghostly marauders prowling around homes. This time from both white and colored families.

And there was one outstanding fact, frightening, indeed, though at first we could not believe that it meant very much, or that it had any connection with this weird affair. In the residential suburb of Paget, across the harbor from Hamilton, a young white girl, named Miss Arton, had vanished. Mr. Dorrance turned from the telephone after listening to the details and faced us with white face and trembling hands, his expression more perturbed and solemn than ever before.

"It means nothing, of course. It cannot mean anything."

"What, father?" Jane demanded. "Something about Eunice?"

"Yes. You know her, Bob—you played tennis down there with her last week. Eunice Arton."

I remembered her. A Bermuda girl; a beauty, second to none in the islands, save perhaps Jane herself. Jane and Don had known her for years.

"She's missing," Mr. Dorrance added. He flashed us a queer look and we stared at him blankly. "It means nothing, of course," he added. "She's been gone only an hour."

But we all knew that it did mean something. For myself I recall a chill of inward horror; a revulsion as though around me were pressing unknown things; unseeable, imponderable things menacing us all.

"Eunice missing! But father, how missing?"

He put his arm around Jane. "Don't look so frightened, my dear child."

He held her against him. If only all of us could have anticipated the events of the next few days. If only we could have held Jane, guarded her, as her father was affectionately holding her now!

DON exclaimed, "But the Chief of Police gave you details?"

"There weren't many to give." He lighted a cigarette and smiled at his trembling hands. "I don't know why I should feel this way, but I do. I suppose—well, it's what you have told me to-night. I don't understand it—I can't think it was all your imagination."

"But that girl, Eunice," I protested.

"Nothing—except she isn't at home where she should be. At eleven o'clock she told her parents she was going to retire. Presumably she went to her room. At eleven-thirty her mother passed her door. It was ajar and a bedroom light was lighted. Mrs. Arton opened the door to say good night to Eunice. But the girl was not there."

He stared at us. "That's all. There is so much hysteria in the air now, that Mr. Arton was frightened and called upon the police at once. The Artons have been telephoning to everyone they know. It isn't like Eunice to slip out at night—or is it, Jane?"

"No," said Jane soberly. "And she's gone? They didn't hear any sound from her?" A strange, frightened hush came upon Jane's voice. "She didn't—scream from her bedroom? Anything like that?"

"No, he said not. Jane, dear, you're thinking more horrible things. She'll be found in the morning, visiting some neighbor or something of the kind."

But she was not found. Bermuda is a small place. The islands are so narrow that the ocean on both sides is visible from almost everywhere. It is only some twelve miles from St. Georges to Hamilton, and another twelve miles puts one in remote Somerset. By noon of the next day it was obvious that Eunice Arton was quite definitely missing.

THIS next day was May 15th—the first of the real terror brought by the White Invaders. But we did not call them that yet; they were still the "ghosts." Bermuda was seething with terror. Every police station was deluged with reports of the ghostly apparitions. The white figures of men—in many instances, several figures together—had been seen during the night in every part of the islands. A little band of wraiths had marched down the deserted main street of Hamilton. It was nearly dawn. A few colored men, three or four roistering visitors, and two policemen had seen them. They had appeared down at the docks and had marched up the slope of the main street.

The stories of eye-witnesses to any strange event always are contradictory. Some said this band of ghostly men marched on the street level; others said they were below it, walking with only their heads above the road surface and gradually descending. In any event the frightened group of onlookers scattered and shouted until the whole little street was aroused. But by then the ghosts had vanished.

There were tales of prowlers around houses. Dogs barked in the night, frantic with excitement, and then shivered with terror, fearful of what they could sense but not see.

In Hamilton harbor, moored at its dock, was a liner ready to leave for New York. The deck watch saw ghosts walking apparently in mid-air over the moonlit bay, and claimed that he saw the white figure of a man pass through the solid hull-plates of the ship. At the Gibbs Hill Lighthouse other apparitions were seen; and the St. David Islanders saw a group of distant figures seemingly a hundred feet or more beneath the beach—a group, heedless of being observed; busy with some activity; dragging some apparatus, it seemed. They pulled and tugged at it, moving it along with them until they were lost to sight, faded in the arriving dawn and blurred by the white line of breakers on the beach over them.

The tales differed materially in details. But nearly all mentioned the dark helmets of strange design, the white, tightly fitting garments, and many described the dark thread-like wires looped along the arms and legs, running up into the helmet, and back across the chest to converge at the belt where there was a clock-like dial-face.

THE ghostly visitors seemed not aggressive. But Eunice Arton was missing; and by noon of May 15th it was apparent that several other white girls had also vanished. All of them were under twenty, all of prominent Bermuda families, and all of exceptional beauty.

By this time the little government was in chaos. The newspapers, by government order, were suppressed. The cable station voluntarily refused to send press dispatches to the outside world. Don, Jane and I, through Mr. Dorrance's prominence, had all the reports; but to the public it was only known by whispered, garbled rumor. A panic was impending. The New York liner, that morning of May 15th, was booked beyond capacity. An English ship, anchored out in the open channel outside Hamilton harbor, received passengers up to its limit and sailed.

The shops of St. Georges and Hamilton did not open that morning of May 15th. People gathered in the streets—groups of whites and blacks—trying to learn what they could, and each adding his own real or fancied narrative to the chaos.

Although there had seemed so far no aggression from the ghosts—our own encounter with the apparition being typical of them all—shortly after noon of the 15th we learned of an event which changed the whole aspect of the affair; an event sinister beyond any which had gone before. It had occurred in one of the hotels near Hamilton the previous night and had been suppressed until now.

A young woman tourist, living alone in the hotel, had occupied a bedroom on the lower floor. The storm blinds and windows were open. During the night she had screamed. Guests in nearby rooms heard her cries, and they were also conscious of a turmoil in the woman's room. Her door was locked on the inside, and when the night clerk finally arrived with a pass-key and they entered, they found the room disordered, a wicker chair and table overturned, and the young woman gone, presumably out of the window. She had been a woman of about twenty-five, a widow, exceptionally attractive.

STOLEN by the ghosts? We could think of nothing else. Was that what had happened to Eunice Arton? Did that explain the reported disappearances of the several other girls? Did this ghostly activity have some rational purpose—the stealing of young white women, all of them of unusual beauty? The conclusion was forced upon us, and with it the whole affair took on a complexion shudderingly sinister. It was not a mere panic of the people with which Bermuda now had to cope—not merely an unexplainable supernatural visitation, harmless enough, save that it was terrorizing. This was a menace. Something which had to be met with action.

It would be futile for me to attempt detailing the events of that chaotic day. We had all ridden over to Hamilton and spent the day there, with the little town in a turmoil and events seething around us—a seemingly endless stream of reports of what had happened the night before. By daylight no apparitions were seen. But another night was coming. I recall with an inward sinking of heart I saw the afternoon sun lowering, the sky-blue waters of the bay deepening into purple and the chalk-white little stone houses taking on the gray cast of twilight. Another night was coming.

The government was making the best preparations it could. Every policeman of the island force was armed and ready to patrol through the night. The few soldiers of the garrisons at St. Georges and Hamilton were armed and ready. The police with bicycles were ready to ride all the roads. The half dozen garbage trucks—low-geared motor trucks—were given over to the soldiers for patrol use. The only other automobiles on the islands were those few permitted for the use of the physicians, and there were a few ambulance cars. All of these were turned over to the troops and the police for patrol.

IN the late afternoon an American newspaper hydroplane arrived from New York. It landed in the waters of Hamilton harbor and prepared to encircle the islands throughout the night. And the three or four steamship tenders and the little duty boat which supplied the government dockyards with daily provisions all had steam up, ready to patrol the island waters.

Yet it all seemed so futile against this unknown enemy. Ghosts? We could hardly think of them now as that. Throughout the chaotic day I recall so many wild things I had heard others say, and had myself thought. The dead come to life as living wraiths? A ghost could not materialize and kidnap a girl of flesh and blood. Or could it? Hysterical speculation! Or were these invaders from another planet?

Whatever their nature, they were enemies. That much we knew.

Night fell upon the crowded turmoil of the little city of Hamilton. The streets were thronged with excited, frightened people. The public park was jammed. The hotels and the restaurants were crowded. Groups of soldiers and police on bicycles with electric torches fastened to their handlebars were passing at intervals. Overhead the airplane, flying low, roared past every twenty minutes or so.

The night promised to be clear. The moon would rise, just beyond the full, a few hours after sunset. It was a warm and breathless night, with less wind than usual. Most of the people crowding the streets and the restaurants were in white linen—themselves suggesting the white and ghostly enemy.

MR. DORRANCE was occupied at the Government House. Jane, Don and I had supper in a restaurant on Queen Street. It was nearly eight o'clock and the crowd in the restaurant was thinning out. We were seated near the street entrance where large plate-glass windows displayed a variety of bakery products and confections. Jane had her back to the street, but Don and I were facing it. Crowds were constantly passing. It was near the end of our meal. I was gazing idly through one of the windows, watching the passing people when suddenly I became aware of a man standing out there gazing in at me. I think I have never had so startling a realization. It was a man in white doeskin trousers and blue blazer jacket, with a jaunty linen cap on his head. An abnormally tall, muscular man. And his smooth-shaven, black-browed face with the reflection from the restaurant window lights upon it, reminded me of the apparition we had seen the night before!

"Don! Don't look up! Don't move! Jane, don't look around!" I whispered, almost frantically.

I must have gone white for Don and Jane gaped at me in astonishment.

"Don't do that!" I murmured. "Someone outside, watching us!" I tried to smile. "Hot night, isn't it? Did you get a check, Don?" I looked around vaguely for the waitress, but out of the tail of my eyes I could see the fellow out there still peering in and staring intently at us.

"What is it?" Don whispered.

"Man watching us! See him out there—the right-hand window! Jane, don't look around!"

"Good Lord!" murmured Don.

"Looks like him, doesn't it?"

"Good Lord! But I say—"

"What is it?" murmured Jane. "What is it?"

"Waitress!" I called. "Check, please. There's a man out there, Jane—we're crazy, but he does look like that ghost we saw on the Fort Beach."

If the fellow knew that we had spotted him he gave no sign. He was still apparently regarding the bakery display in the window, but watching us nevertheless. I was sure of that.

The waitress gave us our check. "Nine and six," Don smiled. "Thank you. But didn't you forget that last coffee?"

The colored girl added the extra sixpence, and left us.

"You think that's the same—I say, good Lord—"

DON was speechless. Jane had gone white. The fellow moved to the other window, and Jane had a swift look at him. We all recognized him, or thought we did. What necromancy was this? Had one of the apparitions materialized? Was that ghost we saw, this gigantic fellow in doeskins and blazer who looked like a tourist standing out there at the window? Were these ghosts merely human enemies after all?

The idea was at once terrifying, and yet reassuring. This was a man with whom we could cope with normal tactics. My hand went to the pocket of my blazer where I had a little revolver. Both Don and I were armed—permits for the carrying of concealed weapons had been issued to us this same day.

I murmured, "Jane! There are the Blakinsons over there. Go join them. We'll be back presently."

"What are you going to do?" Don demanded.

"Go out and tackle him—shall we? Have a talk. Find out who he is."

"No!" Jane protested.

"Why not? Don't you worry, Jane. Right here in the public street—and we're both armed. He's only a man."

But was he only a man?

"We'll have a go at it," said Don abruptly. He rose from his seat. "Come on, Jane, I'll take you to the Blakinsons."

"Hurry it up!" I said. "He's leaving! We'll lose him!"

The fellow seemed about to wander on along the street. Don brought Jane over to the Blakinsons' table which was at the back of the restaurant. We left our check with her and dashed for the street.

"Where is he? Do you see him?" Don demanded.

He had gone. But in a moment we saw him, his white cap towering above the crowd down by the drugstore at the corner.

"Come on, Don! There he is!"

We half ran through the crowd. We caught the fellow as he was diagonally crossing the street. We rushed up, one on each side of him, and seized him by the arms.

CHAPTER THREE
Tako, the Mysterious

THE fellow towered head and shoulders over Don, and almost that over me. He stared down at us, his jaw dropping with surprise. My heart was pounding; to me there was no doubt about it now; this heavy-featured handsome, but evil face was the face of the apparition at whom Don had fired as it hung in the air over the Fort Beach path. But this was a man. His arm, as I clutched it, was muscularly solid beneath the sleeve of his flannel jacket.

"I say," Don panted. "Just a minute."

With a sweep of his arms the stranger angrily flung off our hold.

"What do you want?"

I saw, within twenty feet of us, a policeman standing in the street intersection.

"I beg your pardon," Don stammered. We had had no time to plan anything. I put in:

"We thought you were a friend of ours. This night—so much excitement—let's get back to the curb."

We drew the man to the sidewalk as a physician's little automobile with two soldiers in it waded its way slowly through the crowd.

The man laughed. "It is an exciting night. I never have seen Bermuda like this before."

Swift impressions flooded me. The fellow surely must recognize us as we did him. He was pretending friendliness. I noticed that though he seemed not over forty, his close-clipped hair beneath the white linen cap was silver white. His face had a strange pallor, not the pallor of ill health, but seemingly a natural lack of color. And his voice, speaking good English, nevertheless marked him for a foreigner—though of what nation certainly I could not say.

"We're mistaken," said Don. "But you look like someone we know."

"Do I, indeed? That is interesting."

"Only you're taller," I said. "You're not a Bermudian, are you?"

His eyes, beneath the heavy black brows shot me a look. "No. I am a stranger; a visitor. My name——"

HE hesitated briefly; then he smiled with what seemed an amused irony. "My name is Tako. Robert Tako. I am living at the Hamiltonia Hotel. Does that satisfy you?"

I could think of nothing to say. Nor could Don. The fellow added, "Bermuda is like a little ship. I understand your inquisitiveness—one must know everyone else. And who are you?"

Don told him.

"Ah, yes," he smiled. "And so you are a native Bermudian?"

"Yes."

"And you," he said to me, "you are American?"

"From New York, yes."

"That is more interesting. Never have I known an American. You are familiar with New York City?"

"Of course. I was born there."

His contemplative gaze made me shiver. I wondered what Don was planning as an outcome to this. The fellow seemed wholly at ease now. He was lounging against the drug store window with us before him. My eyes were level with the negligee collar of his blue linen shirt, and abruptly I was galvanized into alertness. Just above the soft collar where his movements had crushed it down I saw unmistakably the loop of a tiny black thread of wire projecting upward! Conclusive proof! This was one of the mysterious enemies! One of the apparitions which had thrown all Bermuda into a turmoil stood materialized here before us.

I think that Don had already seen the wire. The fellow was saying nonchalantly,

"And you, Mr. Livingston—are you also familiar with New York City?"

"Yes," said Don. He had gone pale and tight-lipped. I caught his warning glance to me. "Yes," he repeated. "I lived there several years."

"I would like to know you two better. Much better—but not tonight."

He moved as though to take his leave of us. Then he added to Don, "That most beautiful young lady with you in the restaurant—did I not see you there? Is that your sister?"

Don made his decision. He said abruptly, "That's none of your business."

It took the fellow wholly by surprise. "But listen—"

"I've had enough of your insolence," Don shouted.

The man's hand made an instinctive movement toward his belt, but I seized his wrist. And I added my loud voice to Don's. "No, you don't!"

A GROUP of onlookers was at once collecting around us. The giant tried to cast me off, but I clung to him with all my strength. And suddenly we were struggling to keep the fellow from breaking away from us. He muttered a strange-sounding oath.

"Let me go! You fools!"

"Not such fools," Don shouted. "Officer! I say—officer!"

Don's revolver was in his hand; people were pressing around us, but when they saw the revolver they began scattering. The giant made a lunge and broke away from us, heedless that Don might have shot him.

"What's all this? I say, you three, what are you up to?"

The policeman came on a run. A group of soldiers passing on bicycles, flung the machines aside and came dashing at us. The giant stood suddenly docile.

"Officer, these young men attacked me."

"He's a liar!" Don shouted. "Watch him! He might be armed—don't let him get away from you!"

The law surrounded us. "Here's my weapon," said Don. "Bob, give up your revolver."

In the turmoil Don plucked the policeman aside.

"I'm nephew of the Honorable Arthur Dorrance. Take us to your chief. I made that uproar to catch that big fellow."

The name of the Honorable Arthur Dorrance was magic. The policeman stared at our giant captive who now was surrounded by the soldiers.

"But I say—"

"Take us all in and send for Mr. Dorrance. He's at the Government House."

"But I say—That big blighter—"

"We think he's one of the ghosts!" Don whispered.

"Oh, my Gawd!"

With the crowd following us we were hurried away to the police station nearby.

THE sergeant said, "The Chief will be here in a few minutes. And we've sent for Mr. Dorrance."

"Good enough, Brown." It chanced that Don knew this sergeant very well. "Did you search the fellow?"

"Yes. No weapon in his clothes."

I whispered, "I saw a wire under his collar."

"Sh! No use telling that now, Bob."

I realized it. These policemen were frightened enough at our captive. Don added, "Before my uncle and the Chief arrive, let me have a talk with that fellow, will you?"

They had locked him up; and in the excitement of our arrival at the station both Don and I had completely forgotten the wire we had seen at his collar. But we remembered it now, and the same thought occurred to both of us. We had locked up this mysterious enemy, but would the prison bars hold him?

"Good Lord!" Don exclaimed. "Bob, those wires— Sergeant, we shouldn't have left that fellow alone! Is he alone! Come on!"

With the frightened mystified sergeant leading us we dashed along the little white corridor to the windowless cell in which the giant was confined. At the cell-door a group of soldiers lounged in the corridor.

"Smooth talker, that fellow."

"Gor blime me, who is he?"

We arrived with a rush. "Is he in there?" Don shouted. "Open the door, you fellows! See here, you watch him— we've got to get his clothes off. He's got some mechanism—wires and things underneath his clothes!"

"Get out of the way!" ordered the sergeant. "I'll open it!"

There was silence from behind the door. The prisoner had been in the cell no more than a minute or two.

WE burst open the door. The cell was dimly illumined. The figure of the giant stood backed in its further corner. But at the sight of him we all stood transfixed with horror. His shoes, trousers, shirt, jacket and cap lay in a little pile at his feet. He stood revealed in the short tight-fitting silvery garments. The wires were looped about his arms and legs and he had pulled a mesh of them over his head in lieu of a helmet.

He stood regarding us sardonically. And in that instant while we were stricken with the shock of it, I saw that the figure was fading. It was a solid human form no longer! A silvery cast had come upon it. Another second passed; it was visibly growing tenuous, wraithlike! It was melting while we stared at it, until in that breathless instant I realized that the wall behind it was showing through.

A wraith! An apparition! The vision of a ghost standing there, leering at us!

The soldiers had retreated back into the corridor behind us. The sergeant gripped me, and his other hand, wavering with fright, clutched a revolver.

"But it's—it's going!"

Don gasped, "Too late! Sergeant, give me that gun!"

"Wait!" I shouted. "Don't shoot at it!"

The shimmering glowing white figure was slowly moving downward as though floating through the cell-floor. Its own invisible surface was evidently not here but lower down, and it was beginning to drop. I don't know what frenzied courage—if courage it could be called—was inspiring me. I was wholly confused, but nevertheless I struck Don and the sergeant aside and rushed at the thing.

IT was a sensation most horrible. From the waist up it was still above the floor of the cell. My wildly flailing arms went through the chest! But I felt nothing. It was not even like waving aside a mist. There was nothing. I saw my solid fist plunge through the leering ghostly face. I fought wildly, with a panic upon me, against the glowing phosphorescent nothingness of the apparition. My feet were stamping on its chest and shoulders. Then, as it sank lower, only the grinning face was down there.

Panting, and with the cold sweat of horror upon me, I felt Don shoving me aside.

"Too late!"

And then the sergeant's shot rang out. The bullet clattered against the solid stone floor of the cell. The acrid smoke of the powder rolled over us; and cleared in a moment to show us the apparition several feet below the floor level. It seemed to strike its solidity of ground. I saw it fall the last little distance with a rush; land, and pick itself up. And with a last sardonic grin upward at us, the dim white figure ran. Dwindling smaller, dimmer, until in a moment it was gone into the Unknown.

As though a light had struck upon me came the realization.

"Don, this is rational, this thing! Some strange science!"

All day we had been vaguely realizing it. Intangible, but rational enemies were stealing white girls of Bermuda. Invaders from another planet? We had thought it might be that. Certainly it was nothing supernatural. These was not ghosts.

But now came a new realization. "Don! That's another world down there! Another realm! The fourth dimension—that's what it is! These things everybody's calling ghosts—it's the fourth dimension, Don! People of the fourth dimension coming out to attack us!"

And already the real menace had come! At that moment, half a mile away across the harbor on the slope of the little hill in Paget, an army of the White Invaders suddenly materialized, with dull, phosphorescent-green light-beams flashing around the countryside, melting trees and vegetation and people into nothingness!

The attack upon Bermuda had begun!

CHAPTER FOUR
Ambushed!

THE events which I have now to describe are world history, and have been written in many forms and by many observers. I must, however, sketch them in broadest outline for the continuity of this personal narrative of the parts played by my friends and myself in the dire and astounding affair which was soon to bring chaos, not only to little Bermuda but to the great United States as well, and a near panic everywhere in the world.

On this evening of May 15th, 1938, the White Invaders showed themselves for the first time as rational human enemies. The residential suburb of Paget lies across the little harbor from the city of Hamilton. It is a mile or so by road around the bay, and a few minutes across the water by ferry. The island in the Paget section is a mere strip of land less than half a mile wide in most places, with the sheltered waters of the harbor on one side, and the open Atlantic with a magnificent pink-white beach on the other. The two are divided by a razor-back ridge—a line of little hills a hundred feet or so high, with narrow white roads and white stone residences set on the hill-slopes amid spacious lawns and tropical gardens; and with several lavish hotels on the bay shore, and others over the ridge, fronting the beach.

The invaders landed on the top of the ridge. It seemed that, without warning, a group of white-clad men were in a cedar grove up there. They spread out, running along the roads. They seemed carrying small hand-weapons from which phosphorescent-green light-beams flashed into the night.

The first reports were chaotic. A few survivors appeared in Hamilton who claimed to have been very close to the enemy. But for the most part the descriptions came from those who had fled when still a mile or more away. The news spread as though upon the wings of a gale. Within an hour the hotels were emptied; the houses all along the shore and the bayside hill-slope were deserted by their occupants. Boats over there brought the excited people into Hamilton until no more boats were available. Others came madly driving around the harbor road, on bicycles, and on foot—and still others escaped toward distant Somerset.

A THOUSAND people or more came in within that hour. But there were others who did not come—those who were living in the score or two of houses up on the ridge in the immediate neighborhood of where the invaders appeared....

Don and I met Mr. Dorrance at the police station within a few minutes after the news of the Paget attack reached us. We hurried back to the restaurant and found Jane still there with the Blakinsons. Ten minutes later we were all in the Government House, receiving the most authentic reports available.

From the windows of the second floor room where Mr. Dorrance sat with a number of the officials, Don, Jane, and I could see across the harbor and to the ridge where the enemy was operating. It was not much over two miles from us. The huge, slightly flattened moon had risen. The bay and the distant little hills were flooded with its light. We could see, off on the ridge-top, the tiny flashing green beams. But there was no sound save the turmoil of the excited little city around us.

"They don't seem to be moving," Don murmured. "They're right where they were first reported."

It seemed as though the small group of light-beams, darting back and forth, nevertheless originated from one unshifting place. The beams, we realized, must be extremely intense to be visible even these two miles or so, for we could see that they were very small and of very short range—more like a hand-flashlight than anything else. How many of the enemy were there? They were men, we understood: solid, human men garbed in the fashion of the apparitions which had been so widely seen.

The patrolling airplane, connected with us here by wireless telephone, gave us further details. There seemed to be some fifty of the invaders. They stood in a group in what had been a small cedar grove. It was a barren field now; the trees had melted and vanished before the silent blasts of the green light-beams. They had, these beams, seemingly a range of under a hundred feet. The invaders had, at first, run with them along the nearby roads and attacked the nearest houses. Part of those houses were still standing, save for the wooden portion of them which had vanished into nothingness as the green light touched it. The people, too, were annihilated. The airplane pilot had seen a man running near the field trying to escape. The light touched him, clung to him for a moment. There was an instant as he fell that he seemed melting into a ghostly figure; and then he was gone.

FIFTY invaders. But they were human; they could be attacked. When they first appeared, the nature of them still unrealized, a physician's automobile, manned by three soldiers, had been coming along the bay road at the foot of the ridge. The soldiers turned it into a cross road and mounted the hill. Two of them left it, scouting to see what was happening; the other stayed in the car. One of the enemy suddenly appeared. His ray struck the car. Its tires, its woodwork, and fabric and cushions melted and vanished, and the man within it likewise disappeared. Everything organic vanished under the assailing green beam. The other two soldiers fired at the attacker. He was human. He fell as their bullets struck him. Then others of his fellows came running. The two soldiers were driven away, but they escaped to tell of the encounter.

The airplane pilot, half an hour later, flew low and fired down into the group of enemy figures. He thought that one of them fell. He also thought he was out of range of their beams. But a pencil-point of the green light thinned and lengthened out. It darted up to his hundred-and-fifty-foot altitude and caught one of his wings. The plane fell disabled into the bay near the city docks, but the pilot swam safely ashore.

I need not detail the confusion and panic of the government officials who were gathered here in the room where Don, Jane and I stood watching and listening to the excitement of the incoming reports. For quiet little Bermuda the unprecedented situation was doubly frightening. An attack would have to be made upon the invaders. There were only fifty of the enemy; the soldiers and the police could in a few hours be mobilized to rush them and kill them all.

But could that be done? The thing had so many weird aspects, the invaders still seemed so much in the nature of the supernatural, that Mr. Dorrance advised caution. The enemy was now—this was about ten o'clock in the evening—quietly gathered in the little field on the ridge-top. They seemed, with their first attack over, no longer offensive. But, if assailed, who could say what they would do?

AND a thousand unprecedented things to do were pressing upon the harassed officials. Panic-stricken crowds now surged out of all control in the Hamilton streets. Refugees were coming in, homeless, needing care. The soldiers and the police were scattered throughout the islands, without orders of what to do to meet these new conditions.

And new, ever more frightening reports poured in. The telephone service, which links as a local call nearly every house throughout the islands, was flooded with frantic activity. From nearly every parish came reports of half-materialized ghosts. Fifty invaders? There were that many gathered on the Paget hill, but it seemed that there must be a thousand watching apparitions scattered throughout the islands. Harmless, merely frightening, wraiths. But if that little group in Paget were assailed, this other thousand might in a moment cease to be harmless "ghosts."

The astounded Bermuda officials were forced now to accept the realization that this was solid science. Incredible, fantastic, unbelievable—yet here it was upon us. Some unknown, invisible realm co-existed here in this same space. Its inhabitants had found a way to come out.

The government wireless, and the Canadian cables, could no longer withhold such news as this. Bermuda appealed now to Washington and to London for help. Warships would be coming shortly. Passenger liners on the high seas bringing holiday visitors, were turned aside.

The ships in the port of New York would not sail for Bermuda tomorrow.

I think that the outside world would have had jeering publics amused at little Bermuda hysterical over a fancied attack from the fabled fourth dimension. But by midnight this night, the United States at least was in no mood for jeering. A message came—reaching us soon after eleven o'clock, Bermuda time—by cable, through Halifax from Washington. The thing already had passed beyond the scope of the Bermudas. White apparitions were seen on the Atlantic seaboard near Savannah. And then at Charleston; and throughout the night at several other points farther north. None materialized into solidity. But the "ghosts" were seen, appearing, vanishing, and reappearing always farther north.

It was a world menace!

AT about midnight Mr. Dorrance joined Jane, Don and me where we stood by the Government House windows watching the distant motionless group of enemy lights. He was pale and harassed.

"No use for you to stay here," he told us. "Don, you and Bob take Jane home. It's the safest place now."

The reports seemed to indicate that of all the parishes, St. Georges was now most free of the apparitions.

"Go home," he insisted. "You and Bob stay with Jane. Take care of her, lads." He smiled grimly. "We—all the government—may be moving to St. Georges by morning."

"But, father," Jane protested, "what will you do? Stay here?"

"For a while. I'll drive over by daybreak. I'll keep the Victoria. You have your cycles; you three ride over. Be careful, lads. You have your revolvers?"

"Yes," said Don.

We had no time for leave-taking. He was at once called away from us.

We left the Government House shortly after that, got our bicycles and started for the north shore road. Government Hill, where the road climbed through a deep cut in the solid rock, was thronged with carriages, and with cyclists walking up the hill. Most of the traffic was going in one direction—refugees leaving this proximity to the enemy.

We reached the top of the hill, mounted and began the long coast down. In an hour and a half or less we would be home.... Ah, if one could only lift the veil which hides even the immediate future, upon the brink of which we must always stand unseeing!

The north-shore road had the rocky seacoast upon our left—calm moonlit ocean across which in this direction lay the Carolinas some seven hundred miles away. We had gone, perhaps three miles from Hamilton. The road was less crowded here. A group of apparitions had been seen in the neighborhood of the Aquarium, which was ahead of us, and most of the refugees were taking the middle road along Harrington Sound in the center of the island.

But we decided to continue straight on. It was shorter.

"And there will be more police along here," Don reasoned.

Heaven knows we did not feel in immediate danger. Cycling soldiers passed us at frequent intervals, giving us the news of what lay ahead. And we both had revolvers.

WE came presently to the bottom of one of the many steep little hills up which it is difficult to ride. We were walking up the grade, pushing our machines with Jane between us. A group of soldiers came coasting down the hill, but when we were half-way up they had passed out of sight. It chanced at the moment that we were alone on the road. No house was near us. The ocean to our left lay at the bottom of a fifty-foot rocky cliff; to the right was a thick line of oleander trees, heavy with bloom.

Ahead of us, to the right within the line of oleanders, the glowing white figure of an apparition was visible. We stopped, out of breath from the climb, and stood by the roadside.

"See it there?" Don murmured. "Let's wait and watch it a moment."

One may get used to anything. We were not frightened. The figure, no more than twenty feet ahead of us, stood partly within a tree-trunk. It could not materialize there. It was the figure of a man, with helmet and looped wires.

"Not that fellow who called himself Tako," I whispered.

This one was smaller, no larger than Jane, perhaps. He raised his arms as though warning us to stop. We stood gazing at him, undecided whether to retreat or advance. An omnibus carriage coming from St. Georges stopped at the brow of the hill. Its occupants climbed out and began shouting at the apparition, at the same time flinging stones, one of which came bounding past us.

"Hi!" I called. "Stop that! No sense to that!"

SUDDENLY I heard a rustling of the oleanders at my side. We had no warning; our attention was wholly upon the apparition and the men by the carriage on the brow of the hill flinging stones. There was a rustling; the shadowed oleanders parted and figures leaped upon us!

I recall hearing Don shout, and Jane cry out. Our cycles clattered to the road. I fired at an oncoming white figure, but missed. The solid form of a man struck me and I went down, tangled in my wheel. There was an instant when I was conscious of fighting madly with a human antagonist. I was conscious of Don fighting, too. Jane stood, gripped by a man. Four or five of them had leaped upon us.

I had many instant impressions; then as I fought something struck my head and I faded into insensibility. I must have recovered within a moment. I was lying on the ground, partly upon a bicycle.

Don was lying near me. White figures of men with Jane in their midst were standing off the road, partly behind the bushes. They were holding her, and one of them was swiftly adjusting a network of wires upon her. Then, as I revived further, I heard shouts; people were arriving from down the hill. I tried to struggle to my feet, but fell back.

In the bushes the figures—and the figure of Jane—were turning silvery; fading into wraiths. They drifted down into the ground. They were gone.

CHAPTER FIVE
Into the Enemy Camp

"BUT Bob, I won't go back to Government House," Don whispered. "Lord, we can't do that—get in for theories and questions and plans to gather a police squad. Every minute counts."

"What can we do?"

"Break away from these fellows—send Uncle Arthur a message—anything at all; and say we'll be back in half an hour. I tell you, Jane is gone—they've got her. You saw them take her. By now probably, they've got her off there in Paget among them. We've got to do something drastic, and do it now. If the police attacked—suppose Jane is in that Paget group—the first thing they'd do when the police came at them would be to kill her. We can't go at it that way, I tell you."

We were trudging back up Government Hill with a group of soldiers around us. I had revived to find myself not seriously injured; a lump was on my head and a scalp wound where something had struck me. Don had regained consciousness a moment later and was wholly unharmed. His experience had been different from mine. Two men had seized him. He was aware of a sudden puff of an acrid gas in his face, and his senses had faded. But when they returned he had his full strength almost at once.

We realized what had happened. Half a dozen of the enemy were lying in ambush there on the roadside. It was young white girls they were after, and when we appeared with Jane, one of the invaders showed himself as an apparition to stop us, and then the others, fully materialized and hiding in the oleanders, had leaped upon us. They had had only time to escape with Jane, ignoring Don and me where we had fallen. They seemed also not aware of the nature of our weapons for they had not taken our revolvers.

HAD they gone now with Jane into the other realm of the Unknown? Or was she with them, over in Paget now in the little enemy camp there which was defying Bermuda? We thought very possibly it was the latter. The giant who had called himself Tako, who had escaped us in the Police Station, had been driven from our minds by all the excitement which followed. Was that Tako the leader of these invaders? Had he, for some time perhaps, been living as he said in the Hamiltonia Hotel? Scouting around Bermuda, selecting the young girls whom his cohorts were to abduct?

The thoughts made us shudder. He had noticed Jane. He it was, doubtless, who as an apparition had prowled outside Jane's room the night before last. And last night he had followed us to the Fort Beach. And again to-night in the restaurant he had been watching Jane. These men who had captured Jane now might very well carry her to Paget and hand her over to their leader, this giant Tako.

A frenzy of desperation was upon Don and me at the thought.

"But what shall we do?" I whispered.

"Get away from these soldiers, Bob. We've got our revolvers. We'll ride over there to Paget—just the two of us. It's our best chance that way. Creep up and see what's over there. And if Jane is there, we've got to get her, Bob—get her some way, somehow."

We could plan no further than that. But to return to Government House, to face Jane's father with the tale of what had happened, and then become involved in an official attempt to attack with open hostilities the enemy in Paget—that was unthinkable.

AT the foot of Government Hill, with a trumped-up excuse, Don got us away from our escort. The night was far darker now; a gray-white mass of clouds had come up to obscure the moon. We cycled through the outskirts of Hamilton to the harbor road and followed it around the marshy end of the bay and into Paget. There had been at first many vehicles coming in from the beach, but when we passed the intersection and nothing lay ahead of us but the Paget ridge we found the road deserted.

We had had our handle-bar flash-lights turned on, but now we shut them off, riding slowly into the darkness. Don presently dismounted.

"Better leave our wheels here."

"Yes."

We laid them on the ground in a little roadside banana patch. We were no more than a quarter of a mile from the enemy now; the glow of their green beams standing up into the air showed on the ridge-top ahead of us.

"We'll take the uproad," Don whispered. "Shall we? And when we get to the top, follow some path, instead of a road."

"All right," I agreed.

We started on foot up the steep side road which led from the bay shore to the summit of the ridge. The houses here were all dark and deserted, their occupants long since having fled to Hamilton. It was enemy country here now.

We reached the summit and plunged into a cedar grove which had a footpath through it. The green light-beams seemed very close; we could see them in a little group standing motionless up into the darkness of the sky.

"Can't plan," Don whispered. "But we must keep together. Get up as close as we can and see what conditions are."

And see if Jane were here.... It echoed through my head, and I knew it was also Don's guiding thought.

ANOTHER ten minutes. We were advancing with the utmost caution. The cedar grove was almost black. Then we came to the end of it. There was a winding road and two white houses a hundred feet or so apart. And beyond the houses was a stretch of open field, strangely denuded of vegetation.

"There they are, Bob!" Don sank to the ground with me beside him. We crouched, revolvers in hand, gazing at the strange scene. The field had been a cedar grove, but all the vegetation now was gone, leaving only the thin layer of soil and the outcropping patches of Bermuda's famous blue-gray rock. The houses, too, had been blasted. One was on this side of the field, quite near us. Its walls and roof had partially fallen; its windows and door rectangles yawned black and empty, with the hurricane shutters and the wooden window casements gone and the panes shattered into a litter of broken glass.

But the house held our attention only a moment. Across the two-hundred-foot field we could plainly see the invaders—forty or fifty men's figures dispersed in a little group. It seemed a sort of encampment. The green light beams seemed emanating from small hand projectors resting now on the ground. The sheen from them gave a dull lurid-green cast to the scene. The men were sitting about in small groups. And some were moving around, seemingly assembling larger apparatus. We saw a projector, a cylindrical affair, which half a dozen of them were dragging.

"Bob! Can you make out—back by the banana grove—captives? Look!"

THE encampment was at the further corner of the naked field. A little banana grove joined it. We could see where the enemy light had struck, partially melting off some of the trees so that now they stood leprous. In the grove were other figures of men, and it seemed that among them were some girls. Was Jane there among those captives?

"We've got to get closer," I whispered. "Don, that second house—if we could circle around and get there. From the corner of it, we'd be hidden."

"We'll try it."

The farther house was also in ruins. It stood near the back edge of the naked field and was within fifty feet of the banana grove. We circled back, and within ten minutes more were up against the broken front veranda of the house.

"No one here," Don whispered.

"No, evidently not."

"Let's try getting around the back and see them from the back corner."

We were close enough now to hear the voices in the banana grove. The half-wrecked house against which we crouched was a litter of stones and broken glass. It was black and silent inside.

"Don, look!"

Sidewise across the broken veranda the group of figures in the field were partly visible. We saw ghostly wraiths now among them—apparitions three or four feet above the ground. They solidified and dropped to earth, with their comrades gathering over them. The babble of voices in a strange tongue reached us. New arrivals materializing!

But was Jane here? And Tako, the giant? We had seen nothing of either of them. These men seemed all undersized rather than gigantic. We were about to start around the corner of the veranda for a closer view of the figures in the grove, when a sound near at hand froze us. A murmur of voices! Men within the house!

I PULLED Don flat to the ground against the stone steps of the porch. We heard voices; then footsteps. A little green glow of light appeared. We could see over the porch floor into the black yawning door rectangle. Two men were moving around in the lower front room, and the radiation from their green lights showed them plainly. They were small fellows in white, tight-fitting garments, with the black helmet and the looped wires.

"Don, when they come out—" I murmured it against his ear. "If we could strike them down without raising an alarm, and get those suits—"

"Quiet! They're coming!"

They extinguished their light. They came down the front steps, and as they reached the ground and turned aside Don and I rose up in the shadows and struck at them desperately with the handles of our revolvers. Don's man fell silently. Mine was able to ward off the blow; he whirled and flashed on his little light. But the beam missed me as I bent under it and seized him around the middle, reaching up with a hand for his mouth. Then Don came at us, and under his silent blow my antagonist wilted.

We had made only a slight noise; there seemed no alarm.

"Get them into the house," Don murmured. "Inside; someone may come any minute."

We dragged them into the dark and littered lower room. We still had our revolvers, and now I had the small hand-projector of the green light-beam. It was a strangely weightless little cylinder, with a firing mechanism which I had no idea how to operate.

In a moment we had stripped our unconscious captives of their white woven garments. In the darkness we were hopelessly ruining the mechanism of wires and dials. But we did not know how to operate the mechanism in any event; and our plan was only to garb ourselves like the enemy. Thus disguised, with the helmets on our heads, we could get closer, creep among them and perhaps find Jane....

The woven garments which I had thought metal, stretched like rubber and were curiously light in weight. I got the impression now that the garments, these wires and disks, the helmet and the belt with its dial-face—all this strange mechanism and even the green-ray projector weapon—all of it was organic substance. And this afterward proved to be the fact. (1) (*Footnotes on pg. 202*)

We were soon disrobed and garbed in the white suits of our enemies. The jacket and trunks stretched like rubber to fit us.

"Can't hope to get the wires right," Don whispered. "Got your helmet?"

"Yes. The belt fastens behind, Don."

"I know. These accursed little disks, what are they?"

We did not know them for storage batteries as yet. They were thin flat circles of flexible material with a cut in them so that we could spring the edges apart and clasp them like bracelets at intervals on our arms and legs. The wires connected them, looped up to the helmet, and down to the broad belt where there was an indicator-dial in the middle of the front. (2) (footnotes on page 202)

WE worked swiftly and got the apparatus on somehow. The wires, broken and awry, would not be noticed in the darkness.

"Ready, Don?"

"Yes. I—I guess so."

"I've got this light cylinder, but we don't know how to work it."

"Carry it openly in your hand. It adds to the disguise." There was a note of triumph in Don's voice. "It's dark out there—only the green glow. We'll pass for them, Bob, at a little distance anyway. Come on."

We started out of the room. "You can hide your revolver in the belt—there seems to be a pouch."

"Yes."

We passed noiselessly to the veranda. Over our bare feet we were wearing a sort of woven buskin which fastened with wires to the ankle disks.

"Keep together," Don whispered. "Take it slowly, but walk openly—no hesitation."

My heart was pounding, seemingly in my throat, half-smothering me. "Around the back corner of the house," I whispered. "Then into the banana grove. Straighten."

"Yes. But not right among them. A little off to one side, passing by as though we were on some errand."

"If they spot us?"

"Open fire. Cut and run for it. All we can do, Bob."

Side by side we walked slowly along the edge of the house. At the back corner, the small banana grove opened before us. Twenty feet away, under the spreading green leaves of the trees a dozen or so men were working over apparatus. And in their center a group of captive girls sat huddled on the ground. Men were passing back and forth. At the edge of the trees, by the naked field, men seemed preparing to serve a meal. There was a bustle of activity everywhere; a babble of strange, subdued voices.

WE were well under the trees now. Don, choosing our route, was leading us to pass within ten or fifteen feet of where the girls were sitting. It was dark here in the grove; the litter of rotted leaves on the soft ground scrunched and swished under our tread.

There was light over by the girls. I stared at their huddled forms; their white, terrified faces. Girls of Bermuda, all of them young, all exceptionally pretty. I thought I recognized Eunice Arton. But still it seemed that Jane was not here.... And I saw men seated watchfully near them—men with cylinder weapons in their hands.

Don occasionally would stoop, poking at the ground as though looking for something. He was heading us in a wide curve through the grove so that we were skirting the seated figures. We had already been seen, of course, but as yet no one heeded us. But every moment we expected the alarm to come. My revolver was in the pouch of my belt where I could quickly jerk it out. I brandished the useless light cylinder ostentatiously.

"Don!" I gripped him. We stopped under a banana tree, half hidden in its drooping leaves. "Don—more of them coming!"

Out in the empty field, apparitions of men were materializing. Then we heard a tread near us, and stiffened. I thought that we were discovered. A man passed close to us, heading in toward the girls. He saw us; he raised a hand palm outward with a gesture of greeting and we answered it.

FOR another two or three minutes we stood there, peering, searching for some sign of Jane.... Men were distributing food to the girls now.

And then we saw Jane! She was seated alone with her back against a banana tree, a little apart from the others. And near her was a seated man's figure, guarding her.

"Don! There she is! We can get near her! Keep on the way we were going. We must go in a wide curve to come up behind her."

We started forward again. We were both wildly excited; Jane was at the edge of the lighted area. We could come up behind her; shoot her guard; seize her and dash off.... I saw that the mesh of wires, disks and a helmet were on Jane....

Don suddenly stumbled over something on the ground. A man who had been lying there, asleep perhaps, rose up. We went sidewise, and passed him.

But his voice followed us. Unintelligible, angry words.

"Keep on!" I murmured. "Don't turn!"

It was a tense moment. The loud words brought attention to us. Then there came what seemed a question from someone over by the girls. We could not answer it. Then two or three other men shouted at us.

Don stopped, undecided.

"No!" I whispered. "Go ahead! Faster Don! It's darker ahead."

We started again. It seemed that all the camp was looking our way. Voices were shouting. Someone called a jibe and there was a burst of laughter. And from behind us came a man's voice, vaguely familiar, with a sharp imperative command.

Should we run? Could we escape now, or would a darting green beam strike us? And we were losing our chance for Jane.

Desperation was on me. "Faster, Don!"

The voice behind us grew more imperative. Then from nearby, two men came running at us. An uproar was beginning. We were discovered!

DON'S revolver was out. It seemed suddenly that men were all around us. From behind a tree-trunk squarely ahead a figure appeared with leveled cylinder. The ground leaves were swishing behind us with swiftly advancing footsteps.

"Easy, Bob!"

Don found his wits. If he had not at that moment we would doubtless have been annihilated in another few seconds. "Bob, we're caught—don't shoot!"

I had flung away the cylinder and drawn my revolver; but Don shoved down my extended hand and held up his own hand.

"We're caught!" He shouted aloud. "Don't kill us! Don't kill us!"

It seemed that everywhere we looked was a leveled cylinder. I half turned at the running footsteps behind us. A man's voice called in English.

"Throw down your weapons! Down!"

Don cast his revolver away, and mine followed. I was aware that Jane had recognized Don's voice, and that she was on her feet staring in our direction with horrified eyes.

The man from behind pounced upon us. It was the giant, Tako.

"Well, my friends of the restaurant! The American who knows New York City so well! And the Bermudian! This is very much to my liking. You thought your jail would imprison me, did you not?"

He stood regarding us with his sardonic smile, while our captors surrounded us, searching our belts for other weapons. And he added, "I was garbed like you when we last met. Now you are garbed like me. How is that?"

THEY led us into the lighted area of the grove. "The American who knows New York City so well," Tako added. "And the Bermudian says he knows it also. It is what you would call an affair of luck, having you here."

He seemed highly pleased. He gazed at us smilingly. We stood silent while the men roughly stripped the broken wires and disks from us. They recognized the equipment. There was a jargon of argument in their strange guttural language. Then at Tako's command three of them started for the house.

Jane had cried out at sight of us. Her captor had ordered her back to her seat by the tree.

"So?" Tako commented. "You think silence is best? You are wise. I am glad you did not make us kill you just now. I am going to New York and you shall go with me; what you know of the city may be of help. We are through with Bermuda. There are not many girls here. But in the great United States I understand there are very many. You shall help us capture them."

Don began, "The girl over there——"

"Your sister? Your wife? Perhaps she knows something of New York and its girls also. We will keep her close with us. If you three choose to help me, you need have no fear of harm." He waved aside the men with imperious commands. "Come, we will join this girl of yours. She is very pretty, is she not? And like you—not cowardly. I have not been able to make her talk at all."

The dawn of this momentous night was at hand when, with the networks of wires and disks properly adjusted upon us, Tako took Jane, Don and me with him into the Fourth Dimension.

Strange transition! Strange and diabolical plot which now was unfolded to us! Strangely fantastic, weird journey from this Bermuda hilltop through the Unknown to the city of New York!

CHAPTER SIX
The Attack upon New York

I MUST sketch now the main events following this night of May 15th and 16th as the outside world saw them. The frantic reports from Bermuda were forced into credibility by the appearance of apparitions at many points along the Atlantic seaboard of the southern States. They were sporadic appearances that night. No attacks were reported. But in all, at least a thousand wraithlike figures of men must have been seen. The visitations began at midnight and ended with dawn. To anyone, reading in the morning papers or hearing from the newscasters that "ghosts" were seen at Savannah, the thing had no significance. But in Washington, where officials took a summary of all the reports and attempted an analysis of them, one fact seemed clear. The wraiths were traveling northward. It could almost be fancied that this was an army, traveling in the borderland of the Unknown. Appearing momentarily as though coming out to scout around and see the contour and the characteristics of our realm; disappearing again into invisibility, to show themselves in an hour or so many miles farther north.

The reports indicated also that it was not one group of the enemy, but several—and all of them traveling northward. The most northerly group of them by dawn showed itself up near Cape Hatteras.

The news, when it was fully disseminated that next day, brought a mingling of derision and terror from the public. The world rang with the affair. Remote nations, feeling safe since nothing of the kind seemed menacing them, were amused that distant America, supposedly so scientifically modern, should be yielding to superstition worthy only of the Middle Ages. The accounts from Bermuda were more difficult to explain. And England, with Bermuda involved, was not skeptical; as a matter of fact, the British authorities were astonished. Warships were starting for Bermuda; and that morning of May 16th, with the passenger lines in New York not sailing for Bermuda, American warships were ordered to Hamilton. The menace, whatever it was, would soon be ended.

THAT was May 16th. Another night passed, and on May 17th the world rang with startled horror and a growing terror. Panics were beginning in all the towns and cities of the American seaboard north of Cape Hatteras. It was no longer a matter of merely seeing "ghosts." There had been real attacks the previous night.

There had been a variety of incidents, extraordinarily horrifying—so diverse, so unexpected that they could not have been guarded against. It was a dark night, an area of low pressure with leaden storm-clouds over all the Atlantic coastal region, from Charleston north to the Virginia Capes. A coastal passenger ship off Hatteras sent out a frantic radio distress call. The apparitions of men had suddenly been seen in mid-air directly in the ship's course. The message was incoherent; the vessel's wireless operator was locked in his room at the transmitter, wildly describing an attack upon the ships.

The white apparitions—a group of twenty or thirty men—had been marching in mid-air when the ship sighted them directly over its bow. In the darkness of the night they were only a hundred feet ahead when the lookout saw them. In a moment the vessel was under them, and they began materializing.... The account grew increasingly incoherent. The figures materialized and fell to the deck, picked themselves up and began running about the ship, attacking with little green light-beams. The ship's passengers and crew vanished, obliterated; annihilated. It seemed that young women among the passengers were being spared. The ship was melting—the wooden decks, all the wooden super-structure melting.... A few moments of fantastic horror, then the distress call died into silence as doubtless the green light-beams struck the operator's little cabin.

THAT vessel was found the next day, grounded on the shoals off Hatteras. The sea was oily and calm. It lay like a gruesome shell, as though some fire had swept all its interior. Yet not fire either, for there were no embers, no ashes. Diseased, leprous, gruesomely weird with parts of its interior intact and other parts obliterated. And no living soul was upon it save one steward crouching in a lower cabin laughing with madness which the shock of what he had seen brought upon him.

On land, a railroad train in Virginia had been wrecked, struck apparently by a greenish ray. And also in Virginia, during the early evening in a village, an outdoor festival at which there were many young girls was attacked by apparitions suddenly coming into solidity. The report said that thirty or more young girls were missing. The little town was in chaos.

And the chaos, that next day, spread everywhere. It was obvious now that the enemy was advancing northward. In Washington, Baltimore, Philadelphia, panics were beginning. New York City was seething with excitement.

People were leaving all the towns and cities of the area. An exodus north and westward. In New York, every steamship, airplane and railroad train was crowded with departing people. The roads to Canada and to the west were thronged with outgoing automobiles.

But it was only a small part of the millions who remained. And the transportation systems were at once thrown into turmoil, with the sudden frantic demands threatening to break them down. And then a new menace came to New York. Incoming food supplies for its millions crowded into that teeming area around Manhattan, were jeopardized. The army of men engaged in all the myriad activities by which the great city sustained itself were as terrified as anyone else. They began deserting their posts. And local communication systems went awry. The telephones, the lights, local transportation—all of them began limping, threatening to break.

TREMENDOUS, intricate human machine by whose constant activity so many millions are enabled to live so close together! No one could realize how vastly interwoven are a million activities which make life in a great city comfortable and safe until something goes wrong! And one wrong thing so swiftly affects another! As though in a vastly intricate mechanism little cogs were breaking, and the breaks spreading until presently the giant fly-wheels could no longer turn.

If the startled Federal and State officials could have foreseen even the events of the next forty-eight hours they would have wanted New York City deserted of the population. But that was impossible. Even if everyone could have been frightened into leaving, the chaos of itself would have brought death to untold thousands.

As it was, May 17th and 18th showed New York in a growing chaos. Officials now were wildly trying to stem the panics, trying to keep organized the great machines of city life.

It is no part of my plan for this narrative to try and detail the events in New York City as the apparitions advanced upon it. The crowded bridges and tunnels; the traffic and transportation accidents; the failure of the lights and telephones and broadcasting systems; the impending food shortage; the breaking out of disease from a score of causes; the crushed bodies lying in the streets where frantic mobs had trampled them and no one was available to take them away. The scenes beggar description.

AND in all this the enemy had played no part save that of causing terror. Warships gathered in New York harbor were impotent. State troops massed in New Jersey, across the Hudson from New York, and in Putnam and Westchester Counties, were powerless to do more than try and help the escaping people since there was no enemy of tangible substance to attack. Patrolling airplanes, armed with bombs, were helpless. The white apparitions were gathering everywhere in the neighborhood of New York City. But they remained only apparitions, imponderable wraiths, non-existent save that they could be dimly seen. And even had they materialized, no warships could shell the city, for millions of desperate people were still within it trying to get away.

The news from little Bermuda was submerged, unheeded, in this greater catastrophe. But on the night of May 17th when the American warships arrived off Hamilton, the Paget invaders were gone.

The menace in Bermuda was over; it was the great New York City which was menaced now. The apparitions which had advanced from the south were suddenly joined by a much more numerous army. On the night of May 19th it had reached New York. Two or three thousand glowing white shapes were apparent, with yet other thousands perhaps hovering just beyond visibility. They made no attack. They stood encamped on the borderland of the Unknown realm to which they belonged. Busy with their preparations for battle and watching the stricken city to which already mere terror had brought the horror of disease and death.

It seemed now that this Fourth Dimension terrain co-existing within in the space of New York City, must be a tumbled, mountainous region of crags and spires, and yawning pits, ravines and valley depths. Jagged and precipitous indeed, for there were apparitions encamped in the air above Manhattan and harbor—higher in altitude than the Chrysler or the Empire State towers. Other wraiths showed in a dozen places lower down—some within the city buildings themselves. And yet others were below ground, within the river waters, or grouped seemingly a hundred feet beneath the street levels.

Fantastic army of wraiths! In the daylight they almost faded, but at night they glowed clearly. Busy assembling their weapons of war. Vanishing and reappearing at different points. Climbing or descending the steep cliffs and crags of their terrain to new points of vantage; and every hour with their numbers augmenting. And all so silent! So grimly purposeful, and yet so ghastly silent!

It was near midnight of May 19th when the wraiths began materializing and the attack upon New York City began!

CHAPTER SEVEN
The Invisible World

TAKO showed us how to operate the transition mechanism. The little banana grove on the Bermuda hilltop began fading. There was a momentary shock; a reeling of my head; a sudden sense of vibration within me. And then a feeling of lightness, weightlessness; and freedom, as though all my earthly life I had been shackled, but now was free.

The thing was at first terrifying, gruesome; but in a moment those feelings passed and the weightless freedom brought an exuberance of spirit.

Don and I were sitting with Jane between us, and the figure of Tako fronting us. I recall that we clung together, terrified. I closed my eyes when the first shock came, but opened them again to find my head steadying. Surprising vista! I had vaguely fancied that Tako, Jane and Don would be sitting here dissolving into apparitions. But my hands on Jane's arm felt it as solid as before. I stared into her face. It was frightened, white and set, but smiling at me.

"You all right, Bob? It's not so difficult, is it?"

She had endured this before. She reached out her hands, one to Don and one to me.

"We're dropping. I don't think it's far down, but be careful. Straighten your legs under you."

We seemed unchanged; Don and Jane were the same in aspect as before, save the color of their garments seemed to have faded to a gray. It was the Bermuda hilltop which to our vision was changing. The grove was melting, turning from green and brown to a shimmering silver. We now looked upon ghostly, shadowy trees; fading outlines of the nearby house; the nearby figures of Tako's men and the group of captive girls—all shadowy apparitions. The voices were fading; a silence was falling upon us with only the hum of the mechanism sounding in my ears.

I FELT with a shock of surprise that I was no longer seated on the ground. I seemed, for an instant floating, suspended as though perhaps immersed in water. The sweep of the ground level was a vague shadowy line of gray, but my legs had dropped beneath it. I was drifting down, sinking, with only Jane's hand to steady me.

"Thrust your feet down," she murmured. "A little fall. We want to land on our feet."

The imponderable ground of the banana grove was rising. We dropped, as though we were sinking in water. But we gathered speed; we felt a weight coming to our bodies. At last we fell; my feet struck a solid surface with a solid impact. Don and I lost our balance, but Jane steadied us. We were standing upon a dark rock slope, steeply inclined.

"Off with the current!" came Tako's voice. "The belt switch—throw it back!"

I found the little lever. The current went off. There had been a moment when the spectral shadows of my own world showed in the air above me. But we passed their visible limits and they faded out of sight.

We were in the realm of the Fourth Dimension. Outdoors, in a region of glowing, phosphorescent night....

"THIS way," said Tako. "It is not far. We will walk. Just a moment, you three. I would not have you escape me."

Our revolvers were gone. Being metal, they could not, of actuality, be carried into the transition. We had no light-beam cylinders, nor did we as yet know how to use them. Tako stood before us; he reached to the operating mechanisms under the dial-face at our belts, making some disconnections which we did not understand.

His smile in the semi-darkness showed with its familiar irony. "You might have the urge to try some escaping transition. It would lose you in the Unknown. That would be death! I do not want that."

I protested, "We are not fools. I told you if you would spare us, return us safely to Bermuda when this is over——"

"That you might be of help to me," he finished. "Well, perhaps you will. I hope so. You will do what you can to help, willingly or otherwise; that I know." His voice was grimly menacing. And he laughed sardonically. "You are no fools, as you say. And Jane——" His glance went to her. "Perhaps, before we are through with this, you may even like me, Jane."

Whatever was in his mind, it seemed to amuse him.

"Perhaps," said Jane.

We three had had only a moment to talk together. There had been no possibility of escape. It was obvious to us that Tako was the leader of these invaders; and, whatever they were planning, our best chance to frustrate it was to appear docile. Safety for us—the possibility of later escaping—all of that seemed to lie in a course of docility. We would pretend friendliness; willingness to help.

Tako was not deceived. We knew that. Don, in those two or three hours we were with Tako before starting upon the transition, had said:

"But suppose we do help you in your scheme, whatever it is? There might be some reward for us, eh? If you plan a conquest, riches perhaps—"

Tako had laughed with genuine amusement. "So? You bargain? We are to be real friends—fellow conquerors? And you expect me to believe that?"

YET now he seemed half to like us. And there was Jane's safety for which we were scheming. Tako had been interested in Jane. We knew that. Yet she was at first little more to him than one of the girl captives. He might have left her with those others. But she was with us now, to stay with us upon this journey, and it was far preferable.

"This way," said Tako. "We will walk. It is not far to my encampment where they are preparing for the trip."

It seemed that a vast open country was around us. A rocky, almost barren waste; a mountainous region of steep gray defiles, gorges and broken tumbled ravines. A void of darkness hung overhead. There were no stars, no moon, no light from above. Yet I seemed presently to see a great distance through the glowing deep twilight. The glow was inherent to the rocks themselves; and to the spare, stunted, gray-blue vegetation. It was a queerly penetrating, diffused, yet vague light everywhere. One could see a considerable distance by it. Dim colors were apparent.

We trod the rocks with a feeling of almost normal body weight. The air was softly warm like a night in the tropics, with a faint breeze against our faces. It seemed a trackless waste here. We mounted an ascending ramp, topped a rise with an undulating plateau ahead of us.

Tako stood a moment for us to get our breath. The air seemed rarefied; we were panting, with our cheeks tingling.

"My abode is there." He gestured to the distant lowland region behind us. We were standing upon a gray hilltop. The ground went down a tumbled broken area to what seemed a lowland plain. Ten miles away—it may have been that, or twice that—I saw the dim outline of a great castle or a fortress. A building of gigantic size, it seemed strangely fashioned with round-shaped domes heaped in a circle around a tower looming in the center. A wall, or a hedge of giant trees, I could not tell, but it seemed as gigantic as the wall of China, and was strung over the landscape in an irregular circle to enclose an area of several square miles, with the castle-fortress in its center. A little city was there, nestled around the fortress—a hundred or two small brown and gray mounds to mark the dwellings. It suggested a little feudal town of the Middle Ages of our own Earth, set here in this trackless waste.

AND I saw, down on the plain, a shining ribbon of river with thick vegetation along its banks. And within the enclosing wall there, was the silvery sheen of a lake near the town; patches of trees, and brownish oval areas which seemed to be fields under cultivation.

"My domain," Tako repeated. There was a touch of pride in his voice. "I rule it. You shall see it—when we are finished with New York."

Again his gaze went to Jane, curiously contemplative. We started walking over the upper plateau level, seemingly with nothing in advance of us save empty luminous darkness. A walk of an hour. Perhaps it was that long. Time here had faded with our Earthly world. It was difficult to gauge the passing minutes—as difficult as to guess at the miles of this luminous distance.

As though the sight of his fortress—his tiny principality, whose inhabitants he ruled with absolute sway—had awakened in Tako new emotions, he put Jane beside him and began talking to us with apparent complete frankness. It must have been an hour, during which he explained this world of his, of which we were destined to have so brief a glimpse, and told us upon what diabolical errand he and his fellows were embarked. I recall that as he talked Jane gripped me in horror. But she managed to smile when Tako smiled at her. He was naively earnest as he told us of his coming conquest. And Jane, with woman's intuition knew before Don and I realized it, that it was to herself, a beautiful girl of Earth, he was talking, seeking her admiration for his prowess.

Tako was what in Europe of the Middle Ages would have amounted to a feudal prince. He was one of many here in this realm; each had his little domain, with his retainers cultivating his land, paying fees to him so that the overlord lived in princely idleness.

SCATTERED at considerable distances, one from the other, these rulers of their little principalities were loosely bound into a general government; but at home each was a law unto himself. They lived in princely fashion, these lords of the castle, as they were called. Among the retainers, monogamy was practiced. The workers had their little families—husband, wife and children. But for the rulers, more than one wife was the rule. Within each castle was a harem of beauties, drawn perforce from the common people. The most beautiful girls of each settlement were trained from childhood to anticipate the honor of being selected by the master for a life in the castle.

They were connoisseurs of woman's beauty, these overlords. By the size of his harem and the beauty and talent of its inmates was an overlord judged by his fellows.

Out of this had grown the principal cause for war in the history of the realm. Beautiful girls were scarce. Raids were made by one lord upon the village and harem of another.

Then had come to Tako the discovery of the great world of our Earth, occupying much of this same space in another state of matter.

"I discovered it," he said with his gaze upon Jane.

"How?" Don demanded.

"It came," he said, "out of our scientific method of transportation, which very soon I will show you. We are a scientific people. Hah!" He laughed ironically. "The workers say that we princes are profligate—that we think only of women and music. But that is not so. Once, many generations ago, we were a tremendous nation, and skilled in science far beyond your own world—and with a population a hundred times what we have now. The land everywhere must have been rich and fertile. There were big cities—the ruins of them are still to be seen.

"AND then our climate changed. There was, for us, a world catastrophe, the cause and the details of which no one now knows very clearly. It sent our cities, our great civilizations into ruins. It left us with this barren waste with only occasional lowland fertile spots which now by heredity we rulers control, each to possess his own.

"But that past civilization gave us a scientific knowledge. Much of it is lost—we are going down hill.

But we have some of it left, and we profligate rulers, as the workers call us, cherish it. But what is the use of teaching it to the common people? We do very little of that. And our weapons of war we keep to ourselves—except when there is a raid and our loyal retainers go forth with us to do battle."

"So you discovered how to get into our Earth world?" Don repeated.

"Yes. Some years ago, and it was quite by chance. At first I experimented alone—and then I took with me a young girl."

Again he smiled at Jane. "Tolla is her name. She is here in our camp where our army is now, starting for New York. You will meet her presently. She loves me very much, so she says. She wants some day to lead my harem. I took her with me into the Unknown—into that place you call Bermuda. I have been there off and on for nearly a year of your Earth time, making my plans for what now is at last coming to pass."

"So that's how you learned our language?" I said.

"Yes. It came easy to me and Tolla. That—and we were taught by two girls whom a year ago I took from Bermuda and brought in here."

"And what became of them?" Jane put in quietly.

"Oh—why, I gave them away," he replied calmly. "A prince whose favor I desired, wanted them and I gave them to him. Your Earth girls are well liked by the men of my world. Their fame has already spread."

HE added contemplatively, "I often have thought how strange it is that your great world and mine should lie right here together—the one invisible to the other. Two or three minutes of time—we have just made the transition. Yet what a void!"

"The scientists of your past civilization," I said, "strange that they did not learn to cross it."

"Do you know that they did not?" he demanded. "Perhaps with secret visitations—"

It brought to us a new flood of ideas. We had thought, up there in St. Georges, that this Tako was a ghost. How could one say but that all or most manifestations of the occult were not something like this. The history of our Earth abounds with superstition. Ghosts—things unexplained. How can one tell but that all occultism is merely unknown science? Doubtless it is. I can fancy now that in the centuries of the past many scientists of this realm of the Fourth Dimension ventured forth a little way toward our world. And seeing them, we called them ghosts.

What an intrepid explorer was this Tako! An enterprising scoundrel, fired with a lust for power. He told us now, chuckling with the triumph of it, how carefully he had studied our world. Appearing there, timidly at first, then with his growing knowledge of English, boldly living in Hamilton.

His fame in his own world, among his fellow rulers, rapidly grew. The few Earth girls he produced were eagerly seized. The fame of their beauty spread. The desire, the competition for them became keen. And Tako gradually conceived his great plan. A hundred or more of the overlords, each with his hundred retainers, were banded together for the enterprise under Tako's leadership. An army was organized; weapons and equipment were assembled.

Earth girls were to be captured in large numbers. The most desirable of them would go into the harems of the princes. The others would be given to the workers. The desire for them was growing rapidly, incited by the talk of the overlords. The common man could have more than one wife—two, even three perhaps—supported by the princely master. And Tako was dreaming of a new Empire; increased population; some of the desert reclaimed; a hundred principalities banded together into a new nation, with himself as its supreme leader.

AND then the attack upon Earth had begun. A few Earth girls were stolen; then more, until very quickly it was obvious that a wider area than Bermuda was needed. Tako's mind flung to New York—greatest center of population within striking distance of him. (3) The foray into Bermuda—the materialization of that little band on the Paget hilltop was more in the nature of an experiment than a real attack. Tako learned a great deal of the nature of this coming warfare, or thought he did.

As a matter of actuality, in spite of his dominating force, the capacity for leadership which radiated from him, there was a very naive, fatuous quality to this strange ruler. Or at least, Don and I thought so now. As the details of his plot against our Earth world unfolded to us, what we could do to circumvent him ran like an undercurrent across the background of our consciousness. He knew nothing, or almost nothing of our Earth weapons. What conditions would govern this unprecedented warfare into which he was plunging—of all that he was totally ignorant.

BUT, we were speedily to learn that he was not as fatuous as he at first seemed. These two worlds—

occupying the same space and invisible to each other—
would be plunged into war. And Tako realized that no
one, however astute, of either world could predict what
might happen. He was plunging ahead, quite conscious of
his ignorance. And he realized that there was a vast
detailed knowledge of the Earth world which we had and
he did not. He would use us as the occasion arose to
explain what might not be understandable to him.

I could envisage now so many things of such a
character. The range of warships and artillery. The
weapons a plane might use. The topography of New York
City and its environs.... And the more Tako needed us,
the less we had to fear from him personally. We would
have the power to protect Jane from him—if we could
sufficiently persuade him he needed our good will.
Ultimately we might plunge his enterprise into disaster, and
with Jane escape from him—that too I could envisage as a
possibility.

The mind flings far afield very rapidly! But I recall that
it occurred to me also that I might be displaying many of
the fatuous qualities I was crediting to Tako, by thinking
such thoughts!

I have no more than briefly summarized the many
things Tako told us during that hour while we strode across
the dim rocky uplands toward his mobilized army awaiting
its departure for the scene of the main attack. Some of his
forces had already gone ahead. Several bands of men were
making visual contact with the seacoast of the southern
United States. It was all experimentation. They were
heading for New York. They would wait there, and not
materialize until this main army had joined them.

We saw presently, in the distance ahead of us, a dim
green sheen of light below the horizon. Then it disclosed

itself to be quite near—the reflection of green light from a bowl-like depression of this rocky plateau.

We reached the rim of the bowl. The encampment of Tako's main army lay spread before us.

CHAPTER EIGHT
The Flight through the Fourth Dimension

"THIS is the girl, Tolla," said Tako quietly. "She will take care of you, Jane, and make you comfortable on this trip."

In the dull green sheen which enveloped the encampment, this girl of the Fourth Dimension stood before us. She had greeted Tako quietly in their own language, but as she gazed up into his face it seemed that the anxiety for his welfare turned to joy at having him safely arrive. She was a small girl; as small as Jane, and probably no older. Her slim figure stood revealed, garbed in the same white woven garments as those worn by the men. At a little distance she might have been a boy of Earth, save that her silvery white hair was wound in a high conical pile on her head, and there were tasseled ornaments on her legs and arms.

Her small oval face, as it lighted with pleasure at seeing Tako, was beautiful. It was delicate of feature; the eyes pale blue; the lips curving and red. Yet it was a curious face, by Earth standards. It seemed that there was an Oriental slant to the eyes; the nose was high-bridged; the eyebrows were thin pencil lines snow-white, and above each of them was another thin line of black, which evidently she had placed there to enhance her beauty.

Strange little creature! She was the only girl of this world we were destined to meet; she stood beside Jane, seemingly so different, and yet, we were to learn, so humanly very much the same. Her quiet gaze barely touched Don and me; but it clung to Jane and became inscrutable.

"We will travel together," Tako said. "You make her comfortable, Tolla."

"I will do my best," she said; her voice was soft, curiously limpid. "Shall I take her now to our carrier?"

"Yes."

It gave me a pang to see Jane leave with her; Don shot me a sharp, questioning glance but we thought it best to raise no objection.

"Come," said Tako. "Stay close by me. We will be in the carrier presently."

THERE was an area here in the bowl-like depression of at least half a mile square upon which an assemblage of some five thousand or more men were encamped. It was dark, though an expanse of shifting shadows and dull green light mingled with the vague phosphorescent sheen from the rocks. The place when we arrived was a babble of voices, a confusion of activity. The encampment, which obviously was temporary—perhaps a mobilization place— rang with the last minute preparations for departure. Whatever habitations had been here now were packed and gone.

Tako led us past groups of men who were busy assembling and carrying what seemed equipment of war toward a distant line of oblong objects into which men were now marching.

"The carriers," said Tako. He greeted numbers of his friends, talking to them briefly, and then hurried us on. All these men were dressed similarly to Tako, but I saw none so tall, nor so commanding of aspect. They all stared at Don and me hostilely, and once or twice a few of them gathered around us menacingly. But Tako waved them away. It brought me a shudder to think of Jane crossing this camp. But we had watched Tolla and Jane starting and Tolla had permitted none to approach them.

"Keep your eyes open," Don whispered. "Learn what you can. We've got to watch our chance—" We became aware that Tako was listening. Don quickly added, "I say, Bob, what does he mean—carriers?"

I shrugged. "I don't know. Ask him."

We would have to be more careful; it was obvious that Tako's hearing was far keener than our own. He was fifteen feet away, but he turned his head at once.

"A carrier you would call in Bermuda a tram. Or a train, let us say." He was smiling ironically at our surprise that he had overheard us. He gestured to the distant oblong objects. "We travel in them. Come, there is really nothing for me to do; all is in readiness here."

THE vehicles stood on a level rocky space at the farther edge of the camp. I think, of everything I had seen in this unknown realm, the sight of these vehicles brought the most surprise. The glimpse we had had of Tako's feudal castle seemed to suggest primitiveness.

But here was modernity—super-modernity. The vehicles—there were perhaps two dozen of them—were all apparently of similar character, differing only in size.

They were long, low oblongs. Some were much the size and shape of a single railway car; others twice as long; and several were like a very long train, not of single joined cars, but all one structure. They lay like white serpents on the ground—dull aluminum in color with mound-shaped roofs slightly darker. Rows of windows in their sides with the interior greenish lights, stared like round goggling eyes into the night.

When we approached closer I saw that the vehicles were not of solid structure, but that the sides seemingly woven of wire-mesh—or woven of thick fabric strands. (4)

The army of white figures crowded around the vehicles. Boxes, white woven cases, projectors and a variety of disks and dials and wire mechanisms were being loaded aboard. And the men were marching in to take their places for the journey.

Tako gestured. "There is our carrier."

It was one of the smallest vehicles—low and streamlined, so that it suggested a fat-bellied cigar, white-wrapped. It stood alone, a little apart from the others, with no confusion around it. The green-lighted windows in its sides goggled at us.

WE entered a small porte at its forward pointed end. The control room was here, a small cubby of levers and banks of dial-faces. Three men, evidently the operators, sat within. They were dressed like Tako save that they each had a great round lens like a monocle on the left eye, with dangling wires from it leading to dials fastened to the belt.

Tako greeted them with a gesture and a gruff word and pushed us past them into the car. We entered a low narrow white corridor with dim green lights in its vaulted room. Sliding doors to compartments opened from one side of it. Two were closed; one was partly open. As we passed, Tako called softly:

"All is well with you, Tolla?"

"Yes," came the girl's soft voice.

I met Don's gaze. I stopped short and called:

"Are you all right, Jane?"

I was immensely relieved as she answered, "Yes, Bob."

Tako shoved me roughly. "You presume too much."

The corridor opened into one main room occupying the full ten-foot width of the vehicle and its twenty-foot middle section. Low soft couch seats were here, and a small table with food and drink upon it; and on another table low to the floor, with a mat-seat beside it, a litter of small mechanical devices had been deposited. I saw among them two or three of the green-light hand weapons.

Tako followed my gaze and laughed. "You are transparent. If you knew how to use those weapons, do you think I would leave them near you?"

We were still garbed in the white garments, but the disks and wires and helmet had been taken from us.

"I say, you needn't be so suspicious," Don protested. "We're not so absolutely foolish. But if you want any advice from us on how to attack New York, you've got to explain how your weapons are used."

TAKO seated us. "All in good time. We shall have opportunity now to talk."

"About the trip—" I said. "Are we going to New York City?"

"Yes."

"How long will it take?"

"Long? That is difficult to say. Have you not noticed that time in my world has little to do with yours?"

"How long will it seem?" I persisted.

He shrugged. "That is according to your mood. We shall eat once or twice, and get a little sleep."

One of the window openings was beside us with a loosely woven mesh of wires across it. Outside I could see the shifting lights. Men were embarking in the other vehicles; and the blended noise from them floated in to us.

Questions flooded me. This strange journey, what would it be like? I could envisage the invisible little Bermuda in the void of darkness over us now; or here in this same space around us. No, we had climbed from where we landed in the space close under the Paget hilltop. And we had walked forward for perhaps an hour. The space of Bermuda would be behind us and lower down. This then was the open ocean. I gazed at the solid rocky surface outside our window. Nearly seven hundred miles away must be New York City. We were going there. How? Would it be called flying? Or following this rocky surface?

As though to answer my thoughts Tako gestured to the window. "See. The first carrier starts away."

The carrier lay like a stiff white reptile on the ground. Its doors were closed, and watching men stood back from it.

Don gasped, "Why—it's fading! A transition!"

IT glowed along all its length and grew tenuous of aspect, until in a moment that solid thing which had been solidly resting there on a rock was a wraith of vehicle. A great oblong apparition—the ghost of a reptile with round green spots on its sides. A fading wraith. But it did not quite disappear. Hovering just within visibility, it slowly, silently slid forward. It seemed, without changing its level, to pass partly through an upstanding crag which stood in its path. Distance dimmed it, dwindled it; and in a moment it was gone into the night.

"We will start," said Tako abruptly. "Sit where you are. There will be a little shock, much like the transition coming in from your world." He called, "Tolla, we start."

A signal-dial was on the room wall near him. He rose and pressed its lever. There was a moment of silence. Then the current went on. It permeated every strand of the material of which the vehicle was constructed. It contacted with our bodies. I felt the tingle of it; felt it running like fire through my veins. The whole interior was humming. There was a shock to my senses, swiftly passing, followed by a sense of weightless freedom. But that lightness was an illusion, a comparison with externals only, for the seat to which I clung remained solid, and my body pressed upon it with a feeling of normal weight.

Outside the window, the dark scene of rocks and vehicles and men was fading; turning ghostly, shadowy, spectral. But it did not quite vanish; it held its wraithlike outlines, and in a moment began sliding silently backward. It seemed that we also passed through a little butte of rocks. Then we emerged again into the open; and, as we gathered speed, the vague spectral outlines of a rocky landscape slid past us in a bewildering panorama.

We were away upon the journey. (5)

THERE was little to see during this strange flight. Outside our windows gray shadows drifted swiftly past—a shadowy, ghostly landscape of gray rocks. Sometimes it was below us, so that we seemed in an airship winging above it. Then abruptly it would rise over us and we plunged into it as though it were a mere light-image, a mirage.

Hours passed. For the most part the shadowy void seemed a jagged mountainous terrain, a barren waste.

There were great plateau uplands, one of which rose seemingly thousands of feet over us. And there was perhaps an hour of time when the surface of the world had dropped far away, so far down that it was gone in the distance. Like a projectile we sped level, unswerving. And at last the shadows of the landscape came up again. And occasionally we saw shadowy inhabited domains— enclosing walls around water and vegetation, with a frowning castle and its brood of mound-shaped little houses like baby chicks clustered around the mother hen.

Tako served us with a meal; it was strange food, but our hunger made it palatable. Jane and Tolla remained in their nearby cabin. We did not see them, but occasionally Don or I, ignoring Tako's frown, called out to Jane, and received her ready answer.

Occasionally also, we had an opportunity to question Tako. He had begun tell us the general outline of his plans. The important fact was that the army would mobilize just within visibility of New York.

"Nothing can touch us then," Tako said. "You will have to explain what weapons will be used against me. Particularly the long-range weapons are interesting. But you have no weapons which could penetrate into the shadows of the borderland, have you?"

"No," said Don. "But your weapons—" He tried not to seem too intent. "Look here, Tako, I don't just understand how you intend to conquer New York."

"Devastate it," Tako interrupted. "Smash it up, and then we can materialize and take possession of it. My object is to capture a great number of young women— beautiful young women."

"How?" I demanded. "By smashing up New York? There are thousands of young women there, but you would kill them in the process. Now if you would try some other locality. For instance, I could direct you to open country—"

HE understood my motive. "I ask not that kind of advice. I will capture New York; devastate it. I think then your rulers will be willing voluntarily to yield all the captives I demand. Or, if not, then we will plan to seize them out of other localities."

Don said, "Suppose you tell us more clearly just how you expect to smash New York, as you call it. First, you will gather, not materialized, but only visible to the city."

"Exactly. That will cause much excitement, will it not? Panics—terror. And if we are only wraiths, no weapons of your world can attack us."

"Nor can yours attack the city. Can they?"

He did not at first answer that; and then he smiled. "Our hand light-projectors could not penetrate out from the borderland without losing their force. But we have bombs. You shall see. (6) The bombs alone will devastate New York, if we choose to use them. I have also a long-range projector of the green light-beam. It is my idea, when the city is abandoned by the enemy that we can take possession of some prominent point of vantage. A tall building, perhaps." He smiled again his quiet grim smile. "We will select one and be careful to leave it standing. I will materialize with our giant projector, dominate all the region and then we can barter with your authorities. It is your long-range guns I most fear. When the projector is materialized—and we are ready to bargain—then your airplanes, warships lying far away perhaps, might attack. Suppose now you explain those weapons to me."

FOR an hour or more he questioned us. He was no fool, this fellow; he knew far more of the conditions ahead of him than we realized. I recall that once I said:

"You have never been in New York?"

"No. Not materialized. But I have observed it very carefully."

As a lurking ghost!

"We have calculated," he went on, "the space co-ordinates with great precision. That is how we have been able to select the destination for this carrier now. You cannot travel upon impulse by this method. Our engineers, as you might call them, must go in advance with recording apparatus. Nothing can be done blindly."

It brought to my mind the three pilots now operating our vehicle. I mentioned the lens on their left eyes like a monocle.

"With that they can see ahead of us a great distance. It flings the vision—like gazing along a beam of light—to space-time factors in advance of our present position. In effect, a telescope."

THERE were a few hours of the journey when Don and I slept, exhausted by what we had been through. Tako was with us when we dozed off, and I recall that he was there when we awakened. How much time passed we could not tell.

"You are refreshed?" he said smilingly. "And hungry again, no doubt. We will eat and drink—and soon we will arrive at the predestined time and place."

We were indeed hungry again. And while we were eating Tako gestured to the window. "Look there. Your world seems visible a little."

Just before we slept it had seemed that mingled with the shadows of Tako's world was the gray outline of an ocean surface beneath us. I gazed out at the dim void now. Our flight was far slower than before. We were slackening speed for the coming halt. And I saw now that the shadows outside were the mingled wraiths of two spectral worlds, with us drifting forward between and among them. The terrain of Tako's world was bleaker, more desolate and more steeply mountainous than ever. There were pits and ravines and gullies with jagged mountain spires, cliffs and towering gray masses of rock.

And mingled with it, in a general way coincidental with it in the plane of the same space, we could see now the tenuous shapes of our own world. Vague, but familiar outlines! We had passed Sandy Hook! The ocean lay behind us. A hundred feet or so beneath us was the level water of the Lower Bay.

"Don!" I murmured. "Look there! Long Island off there! And that's Staten Island ahead of us!"

"Almost at our destination," Tako observed. And in a moment he gestured again. "There is your city. Have a good look at your dear New York."

DIAGONALLY ahead through the window we saw the spectres of the great pile of masonry on lower and mid-Manhattan. Spectres of the giant buildings; the familiar skyline, and mingled with it the ghostly gray outlines of the mountains and valley depths of Tako's world. All intermingled! The mountain peaks rose far higher than the tallest of New York's skyscrapers; and the pits and ravines were lower than the waters of the harbor and rivers, lower than the subways and the tubes and the tunnels.

"Another carrier!" Don said abruptly. "See it off there!"

It showed like a great gray projectile coming in level with us. And then we saw two others in the distance behind us. Fantastic, ghostly arrival of the enemy! Weird mobilization here within the space of the doomed New York.

"Can they see us?" I murmured. "Tako, the people down there on Staten Island—can they see us?"

"Yes," he smiled. "Don't you think so? Look! Are not those ships of war? Hah! Gathered already—awaiting our coming!"

I have already given a brief summary of the events of the days and nights just past here in New York. The terror at the influx of apparitions. The panic of the city's teeming millions struggling too eagerly to escape.

It was night now—the night of May 19th. The city was in chaos, but none of the details were apparent to us as we arrived. But we could see, as we drifted with slow motion above the waters of the harbor, that there were warships anchored here, and in the Hudson River. They showed as little spectral dots of gray. And in the air, level with us at times, the wraiths of encircling airplanes were visible.

"They see us," Tako repeated.

They did indeed. A puff of light and up-rolling smoke came from one of the ships. A silent shot. Perhaps it screamed through us, but we were not aware of it.

Tako chuckled. "They get excited, do they not? We strike terror—are they going to fight like excited children?"

WE were under sudden bombardment. Fort Wadsworth was firing; puffs showed from several of the warships; and abruptly a group of ghostly monoplanes dove at us like birds. They went through us, emerged and sped away. And in a moment the shots were discontinued.

"That is better," said Tako. "What a waste of ammunition."

Our direction was carrying us from mid-Manhattan. The bridges to Brooklyn were visible. Beyond them, over New York, mingled with teeming buildings was a mountain slope of Tako's realm. I saw one of our carriers lying on a ledge of it.

A sudden commotion in our car brought our attention from the scene outside. The voices of girls raised in anger. Tolla's voice and Jane's! Then came the sound of a scuffle!

"By what gods!" Tako exclaimed.

We all leaped to our feet. Tako rushed for the door of the compartment with us after him. We burst in upon the girls. They were standing in the center of the little room. One of the chairs was overturned. Jane stood gripping Tolla by the wrists, and with greater strength was forcibly holding her.

As we appeared, Jane abruptly released her, and Tolla sank to the floor and burst into wild sobs. Jane faced us, red and white of face, and herself almost in tears.

"What's the matter?" Don demanded. "What is it?"

But against all our questionings both girls held to a stubborn silence.

CHAPTER NINE
A Woman Scorned

JANE afterward told us just what happened in that compartment of the carrier, and I think that for the continuity of my narration I had best relate it now.

The cubby room was small, not much over six feet wide, and twelve feet long. There was a single small door to the corridor, and two small windows. A couch stood by them; there were two low chairs, and a small bench-like table.

Tolla made Jane as comfortable as possible. Food was at hand; Tolla, after an hour or two served it at the little table, eating the meal with Jane, and sitting with her on the couch where they could gaze through the windows.

To Jane this girl of another world was at once interesting, surprising and baffling. Jane could only look upon her as an enemy. In Jane's mind there was no thought save that we must escape, and frustrate Tako's attack upon New York; and she was impulsive, youthful enough to think something might be contrived.

At all events, she saw Tolla in the light of an enemy who might be tricked into giving information.

Jane admits that her ideas were quite as vague as our own when it came to planning anything definite.

She at first studied Tolla, who seemed as young as herself and perhaps in her own world, was as beautiful. And within an hour or two she was surprised at Tolla's friendliness. They had dined together, gazed through the windows at the speeding shadows of the strange world sliding past; they had dozed together on the couch. During all this they could have been schoolgirl friends. Not captor and captive upon these strange weird circumstances of actuality, but friends of one world. And in outward aspect Tolla could fairly well have been a cultured girl of our Orient.

THEN Jane got a shock. She tried careful questions. And Tolla skillfully avoided everything that touched in any way upon Tako's future plans. Yet her apparent friendliness, and a certain girlish volubility continued.

And then, at one point, Tolla asked:

"Are you beautiful in Bermuda?"

"Why, yes," said Jane. "I guess so."

"I am beautiful in my world. Tako has said so."

"You love him, don't you?" Jane said abruptly.

"Yes. That is true." There was no hint of embarrassment. Her pale blue eyes stared at Jane, and she smiled a little quizzically. "Does it show so quickly upon my face that you saw it at once? I am called Tolla because I am pledged soon to enter Tako's harem."

Upon impulse Jane put her arm around the other girl as they sat on the couch. "I think he is very nice."

But she saw it was an error. The shadow of a frown came upon Tolla's face; a glint of fire clouded her pale, serene eyes.

"He will be the greatest man of his world," she said quietly.

THERE was an awkward silence. "The harem, I am told," Jane said presently, "is one of your customs." She took a plunge. "And Tako told us why they want our

Earth girls. There was one of my friends stolen from Bermuda—"

"And yet you call him very nice," Tolla interrupted with sudden irony. "Girls are frank in our world. But you are not. What did you mean by that?"

"I was trying to be friendly," said Jane calmly. "You had just said you loved him."

"But you do not love him?"

It took Jane wholly back. "Good Heavens, no!"

"But he—might readily love you?"

"I hope not!" Jane tried to laugh, but the idea itself was so frightening to her that the laugh sounded hollow. She gathered her wits. This girl was jealous. Could she play upon that jealousy? Would Tolla perhaps soon want her to escape? The idea grew. Tolla might even some time soon come to the point of helping her escape.

Jane said carefully, "I suppose I was captured with the idea of going into someone's harem. Was that the idea?"

"I am no judge of men's motives," said Tolla curtly.

"Tako said as much as that," Jane persisted. "But not necessarily into his harem. But if it should be his, why would you care? Your men divide their love—"

"I would care because Tako may give up his harem," Tolla interrupted vehemently. "He goes into this conquest for power—for wealth—because soon he expects to rule all our world and band it together into a nation. He has always told me that I might be his only wife—some day—"

SHE checked herself abruptly and fell into a stolid silence. It made Jane realize that under the lash of emotion Tolla would talk freely. But Jane could create no further opportunity then, for Tako suddenly appeared at their door. The girls had been together now some hours. Don and I were at this time asleep.

He stood now at the girl's door. "Tolla, will you go outside a moment? I want to talk to this prisoner alone." And, interpreting the look which both girls flung at him, he added, "The door remains open. If she wants you back, Tolla, she will call."

Without a word Tolla left the compartment. But Jane saw on her face again a flood of jealousy.

Tako seated himself amiably. "She has made you comfortable?"

"Yes."

"I am glad."

He passed a moment of silence. "Have you been interested in the scene outside the window?" he added.

"Yes. Very."

"A strange sight. It must seem very strange to you. This traveling through my world—"

"Did you come to tell me that?" she interrupted.

He smiled. "I came for nothing in particular. Let us say I came to get acquainted with you. My little prisoner—you do not like me, do you?"

She tried to meet his gaze calmly. This was the first time Jane had had opportunity to regard Tako closely. She saw now the aspect of power which was upon him. His gigantic stature was not clumsy, for there was a lean, lithe grace in his movements. His face was handsome in a strange foreign fashion. He was smiling now; but in the set of his jaw, his wide mouth, there was an undeniable cruelty, a ruthless dominance of purpose. And suddenly she saw the animal-like aspect of him; a thinking, reasoning, but ruthless, animal.

"You do not like me, do you?" he repeated.

SHE forced herself to reply calmly, "Why should I? You abduct my friends. There is a girl named Eunice Arton whom you have stolen. Where is she?" (7)

He shrugged. "You could call that the fortunes of war. This is war—"

"And you," she said, "are my enemy."

"Oh, I would not go so far as to say that. Rather would I call myself your friend."

"So that you will return me safely? And also Bob Rivers, and my cousin, Don—you will return us safely as you promised?"

"Did I promise? Are you not prompting words from my lips?"

Jane was breathless from fear, but she tried not to show it.

"What are you going to do with us?" she demanded. There is no woman who lacks feminine guile in dealing with a man; and in spite of her terror Jane summoned it to her aid.

"You want me to like you, Tako?"

"Of course I do. You interest me strangely. Your beauty—your courage—"

"Then if you would be sincere with me—"

"I am; most certainly I am."

"You are not. You have plans for me. I told Tolla I supposed I was destined for someone's harem. Yours?"

It startled him. "Why—" He recovered himself and laughed. "You speak with directness." He suddenly turned solemn. He bent toward her and lowered his voice; his hand would have touched her arm, but she drew away.

"In very truth, ideas are coming to me, Jane. I will be, some day soon, the greatest man of my world. Does that attract you?"

"N-no," she said, stammering.

"I wish that it would," he said earnestly. "I do of reality wish that it would. I will speak plainly, and it is in a way that Tako never spoke to woman before. I have found myself, these last hours, caring very much for your good opinion of me. That is surprising."

SHE stared at him with sudden fascination mingled with her fear. He seemed for this moment wholly earnest and sincere. An attractive sort of villain, this handsome giant, turned suddenly boyish and naive.

"That is surprising," Tako repeated.

"Is it?"

"Very. That I should care what any woman thinks of me, particularly a captive girl—but I do. And I realize, Jane, that our marriage system is very different from yours. Repugnant to you, perhaps. Is it?"

"Yes," she murmured. His gaze held her; she tried to shake it off, but it held her.

"Then I will tell you this: I have always felt that the glittering luxury of a large harem is in truth a very empty measure of man's greatness. For Tako there will be more manly things. The power of leadership—the power to rule my world. When I got that idea, it occurred to me also that for a man like me there might be some one woman—to stand alone by my side and rule our world."

His hand touched her arm, and though she shuddered, she left it there. Tako added with a soft vibrant tenseness. "I am beginning to think that you are that woman."

There was a sound in the corridor outside the door—enough to cause Tako momentarily to swing his gaze. It broke the spell for Jane; with a shock she realized that like a snake he had been holding her fascinated. His gaze came back at once, but now she shook off his hand from her arm.

"Tolla told me you—you said something like that to her," Jane said with an ironic smile.

It angered him. The earnestness dropped from him like a mask. "Oh, did she? And you have been mocking me, you two girls?"

HE stood up, his giant length bringing his head almost to the vaulted ceiling of the little compartment. "What degradation for Tako that women should discuss his heart."

His frowning face gazed down at Jane; there was on it now nothing to fascinate her; instead, his gaze inspired terror.

"We—we said nothing else," she stammered.

"Say what you like. What is it to me? I am a man, and the clatter of women's tongues is no concern of mine."

He strode to the door. From over his shoulder he said, "What I shall do with you I have not yet decided. If Tolla is interested, tell her that."

"Tako, let me—I mean you do not understand—"

But he was gone. Jane sat trembling. A sense of defeat was on her. Worse than that, she felt that she had done us all immeasurable harm. Tako's anger might react upon Don and me. As a matter of fact, if it did he concealed it, for we saw no change in his attitude.

Tolla rejoined Jane within a moment. If Tako spoke to her outside Jane did not know it. But she was at once aware that the other girl had been listening; Tolla's face was white and grim. She came in, busied herself silently about the room.

Jane turned from the window. "You heard us, Tolla?"

"Yes, I heard you! You with your crooked look staring at him—"

"Why, Tolla, I did not!"

"I saw you! Staring at him so that he would think you beautiful! Asking him, with a boldness beyond that of any woman I could ever imagine—asking him if he planned you for his harem!"

SHE stood over Jane, staring down with blazing eyes. "Oh, I heard you! And I heard him telling you how noble are his motives! One woman, just for him!"

"But, Tolla—"

"Do not lie to me! I heard him sneering at me—telling you of this one woman just for him! And you are that woman! Hah! He thinks that now, does he? He thinks he will make you love him as I love him. As I love him! And what does he know of that! What woman's love can mean!"

"Tolla! Don't be foolish. I didn't—I never had any desire to—"

"What do your desires concern me? He thinks he will win you with tales of his conquests! A great man, this Tako, because he will devastate New York!"

This was the fury of a woman scorned. She was wholly beside herself, her words tumbling, incoherent, beyond her will, beyond her realization of what she was saying.

"A great conquest to make you love him! With his giant projector he will subdue New York! Hah! What a triumph! But it is the weapon's power, not his! He and all his army—these great brave and warlike men—why I alone with that weapon could turn—"

She stopped abruptly. The red flush of frenzied anger drained from her cheeks.

Jane leaped to her feet. "What do you mean? With that giant projector—"

But Tolla was standing frozen, with all her anger gone and horror at what she had said flooding her.

"What do you mean, Tolla?" insisted Jane, seizing her. "What could you do with that giant projector?"

"Let me go!" Tolla tried to jerk away.

"I won't let you go! Tell me what you were going to say!"

"Let me go!" Tolla got one hand loose and struck Jane in the face. But Jane again seized the wrist. In the scuffle they overturned a chair.

"I won't let you go until you—"

And then Tako, Don and I, hearing the uproar, burst in upon them. Jane let go her hold, and Tolla broke into sobs, and sank to the floor.

And both of them were sullen and silent under our questioning.

CHAPTER TEN
Weird Battleground!

"WE have it going very well," said Tako, chuckling. "Don't you think so? Sit here by me. We will stay here for a time now."

Tako had a small flat rock for a table. On it he had spread his paraphernalia for this battle—if battle it could be called. Weird contest! Opposing forces, each imponderable to the other so that no physical contact had yet been made. Tako sat at his rock; giving orders to his leaders who came hurrying up and were away at his command; or speaking orders into his sound apparatus; or consulting his charts and co-ordinates, questioning Don and me at times over the meaning of shadowy things we could see taking place about us.

A little field headquarters our post here might have been termed. (8)

We were grouped now around Tako on a small level ledge of rock. It lay on a broken, steeply ascending ramp of a mountainside. The mountain terraces towered back and above us. In front, two hundred feet down, was a valley of pits and craters; and to the sides a tumbled region of alternating precipitous cliffs and valley depths.

Upon every point of vantage, for two or three miles around us, Tako's men were dispersed. To us, they were solid gray blobs in the luminous darkness. The carriers, all arrived now, stood about a mile from us, and save for their guards, the men had all left them. The weapons were being taken out and carried to various points over the mountains and in the valley depths. Small groups of men—some two hundred in a group—were gathered at many different points, assembling their weapons, and waiting for Tako's orders. Messengers toiled on foot between them, climbing, white figures. Signals flashed.

Fantastic, barbaric scene—it seemed hardly modern. Mountain defiles were swarming with white invaders, making ready, but not yet attacking.

WE had had as yet no opportunity of talking alone with Jane since we left the carrier. The incident with Tolla was to us wholly inexplicable. But that it was significant of something, we knew—by Jane's tense white face and the furtive glances she gave us. Don and I were ready to seize the first opportunity to question her.

Tolla, by the command of Tako, stayed close by Jane, and the two girls were always within sight of us. They were here now, seated on the rocks twenty feet from us. And the two guards, whom Tako had appointed at the carrier, sat near us with alert weapons, watching Jane and us closely. (9)

There was just once after we left the carrier, toiling over the rocks with Tako's little cortege to this vantage point on the ledge, that Jane found an opportunity of communicating secretly with us.

"Tolla told me something about the giant projector! Something about how it—"

She could say almost nothing but that. "The projector, Bob, if you can only learn how it—"

Tolla was upon us, calling to attract Tako's attention, and Jane moved away.

THE giant projector! We had it with us now; a dozen men had laboriously carried it up here. Not yet assembled, it stood here on the ledge—a rectangular gray box about the size and shape of a coffin, encased now in the mesh of transition mechanism. Tako intended to materialize us and that box into the city when the time came, unpack and erect the projector, and with its long range dominate all the surrounding country.

Tolla had almost told Jane something about it! Jane was trying to learn that secret. Or she thought we might learn it from Tako. But of what use if we did? We were helpless, every moment under the eyes of guards whose little hand-beams could in a second annihilate us. When, leaving the carrier, Jane had appeared garbed like the rest of us and we had all been equipped with the transition mechanism which we knew well how to use now, the thought came to me of trying to escape. But it was futile. I could set the switches at my belt to materialize me into New York. But as I faded, the weapons of the guards would have been quick enough to catch me. How could Jane, Don and I simultaneously try a thing like that.

"Impossible!" Don whispered. "Don't do anything wrong. Some chance may come, later."

But with that slight transition over, Tako at once removed from our belts a vital part of the mechanism in order to make it impotent.

An hour passed, here on the ledge, with most of the activity of Tako's men incomprehensible to us.

"You shall see very soon," he chuckled grimly, "I can give the signal to attack—all at once. Look there! They grow very bold, these New York soldiers. They have come to inspect us."

IT was night in New York City—about two A.M. of the night of May 19th and 20th. Our mountain ledge was within a store on the east side of Fifth Avenue at 36th Street. We seemed to be but one story above the pavement. The shadowy outlines of a large rectangular room with great lines of show-cases dividing it into wide aisles. I recognized it at once—a jewelry store, one of the best known in the world. A gigantic fortune in jewelry was here, some of it hastily packed in great steel safes nearby, and some of it abandoned in these show-cases when the panic swept the city a few days previously.

But the jewelry of our world was nothing to these White Invaders. Tako never even glanced at the cases, or knew or cared what sort of a store this was.

The shadowy street of Fifth Avenue showed just below us. It was empty now of vehicles and people, but along it a line of soldiers were gathered. Other stores and ghostly structures lay along Fifth Avenue. And five hundred feet away, diagonally across the avenue, the great Empire State Building, the tallest structure in the entire world, towered like a ghostly Titan into the void above us.

This ghostly city! We could see few details. The people had all deserted this mid-Manhattan now. The stores and hotels and office buildings were empty.

A group of soldiers came into the jewelry store and stood within a few feet of us, peering at us. Yet so great was the void between us that Tako barely glanced at them. He was giving orders constantly now. For miles around us his men on the mountains and in the valleys were feverishly active.

BUT doing what? Don and I could only wonder. A tenseness had gripped upon Tako. The time for his attack was nearing.

"Very presently now," he repeated. He gestured toward the great apparition of the Empire State Building so near us.

"I am sparing that. A good place for us to mount the projector—up there in that tall tower. You see where our mountain slope cuts through that building? We can materialize with the projector at that point."

The steep ramp of the mountainside upon which we were perched sloped up and cut midway through the Empire State Building. The building's upper portion was free of the mountain whose peaks towered to the west. We could climb from our ledge up the ramp to the small area where it intersected the Empire State at the building's sixtieth to seventieth stories.

The apparitions of New York's soldiers stood in the jewelry store with futile leveled weapons.

"They are wondering what we are doing!" Tako chuckled.

A dozen of Tako's men, unheeding the apparitions, were now busy within a few hundred feet of us down the rocky slope. We saw at close view, what Tako's army was busy doing everywhere. The men had little wedge-shaped objects of a gray material. The materialization bombs! They were placing them carefully at selected points on the rocks, and adjusting the firing mechanisms. This group near us, which Don and I watched with a fascinated horror, were down in the basement of the jewelry store, among its foundations. There for a moment; then moving out under Fifth Avenue, peering carefully at the spectral outlines of the cellars of other structures.

Then presently Tako called an order. He stood for a moment on the ledge with arms outstretched so that his men, and Don and I and Jane, and the wondering apparitions of the gathered soldiers and New York Police could see him. His moment of triumph! It marked his face with an expression which was utterly Satanic.

Then he dropped his arms for the signal to attack.

CHAPTER ELEVEN
The Devastation of New York

THAT night of May 19th and 20th in New York City will go down in history as the strangest, most terrible ever recorded. The panics caused by the gathering apparitions of the previous days were nearly over now. The city was under martial law, most of it deserted by civilians, save for the dead who still lay strewn on the streets.

Lower and mid-Manhattan were an empty shell of deserted structures, and silent, littered streets, which at night were dark, and through which criminals prowled, braving the unknown terror to fatten upon this opportunity.

Soldiers and police patrolled as best they could all of Manhattan, trying to clear the streets of the crushed and trampled bodies; seeking in the deserted buildings those who might still be there, trapped or ill, or hurt so that they could not escape; protecting property from the criminals who en masse had broken jail and were lurking here.

Warships lay in the harbor and the rivers. The forts on Staten Island and at Sandy Hook were ready with their artillery to attack anything tangible. Airplanes sped back and forth overhead. Troops were marching from outlying points—lines of them coming in over all the bridges.

By midnight of May 19th and 20th there were groups of ghosts visible everywhere about the city. They lurked in the buildings, permeating the solid walls, stalking through them, or down through the foundations; they wandered upon invisible slopes of their own world, climbing up to gather in groups and hanging in mid-air over the city rooftops. In the Hudson River off Grant's Tomb two or three hundred of the apparitions were seemingly encamped at a level below the river's surface. And others were in the air over the waters of the upper bay.

TOWARD midnight, from the open ocean beyond Sandy Hook spectral vehicles came winging for the city. Rapidly decreasing what had at first seemed a swift flight, they floated like ghostly dirigibles over the bay, heading for Manhattan. The forts fired upon them; airplanes darted at them, through them. But the wraiths came on unheeding. And then, gathering over Manhattan at about Washington Square, they faded and vanished.

Within thirty minutes, though the vehicles never reappeared, it was seen that the spectral invaders were now tremendously augmented in numbers. A line of shapes marched diagonally beneath the city streets. Patrolling soldiers in the now deserted subways saw them marching past. The group in the air over the harbor was augmented. In Harlem they were very near the street levels, a mass of a thousand or more strung over an area of forty blocks.

In mid-Manhattan soldiers saw that Tiffany's jewelry store housed the lurking shapes. Some were lower, others higher; in this section around Fifth Avenue and Thirty-fourth Street the apparitions were at tremendously diverse levels. There were some perched high in the air more than half way up the gigantic Empire State Building; and still others off to the west were in the air fifteen hundred feet or more above the Pennsylvania Station.

AT Tiffany's—as indeed in many other places—the soldiers made close visual contact with the apparitions. A patrolling group of soldiers entered Tiffany's and went to the second floor. They reported a seated group of "ghosts," with numbers of white shapes working near them at a lower level which brought them into Tiffany's basement.

The soldiers thought that what was seated here might be a leader. Apparitions rushed up to him, and away. And here the soldiers saw what seemed the wraiths of two girls, seated quietly together, helmeted and garbed like the men. And men seemed watching them.

By one-thirty there was great activity, constant movement of the apparitions everywhere. Doing what? No one could say. The attack, so closely impending now, was presaged by nothing which could be understood.

There was one soldier who at about one-thirty A.M. was watching the spectres which lurked seemingly in the foundations of Tiffany's. He was called to distant Westchester where the harried Army officials had their temporary headquarters this night. He sped there on his motorcycle and so by chance he was left alive to tell what he had seen. The wraiths under Tiffany's were placing little wedge-shaped ghostly bricks very carefully at different points. It occurred to this soldier that they were putting them in spaces coincidental with the building's foundations.

And then came the attack. The materialization bombs—as we knew them to be—were fired. Progressively over a few minutes, at a thousand different points. The area seemed to be from the Battery to Seventy-second Street. Observers in circling airplanes saw it best—there were few others left alive to tell of it.

THE whole thing lasted ten minutes. Perhaps it was not even so long. It began at Washington Square. The little ghostly wedges which had been placed within the bricks of the arch at the foot of Fifth Avenue began materializing; turning solid. From imponderability they grew tangible; demanded free empty space of their own. Wedged and pushed with solidifying molecules and atoms, each demanding its little space and finding none. Encountering other solidity.

Outraged nature! No two material bodies can occupy the same space at the same time!

The Washington Arch very queerly seemed to burst apart by a strangely silent explosion. The upper portion toppled and fell with a clatter of masonry littering the avenue and park.

Then a house nearby went down; then another. Everything seemed to be crumbling, falling. That was the beginning. Within a minute the chaos spread, running over the city like fire on strewn gasoline. Buildings everywhere came crashing down. The street heaved up, cracking apart in long jagged lines of opening rifts as though an earthquake were splitting them. The subways and tubes and tunnels yawned like black fantastic chasms crossed and littered by broken girders.

The river waters heaved with waves lashed white as the great bridges fell into them; and sucked down and closed again with tumultuous whirlpools where the water had rushed into the cracked tunnels of the river bed.

OF the towering skyscrapers the Woolworth was the first to crumble; it split into sections as it fell across the wreckage which already littered City Hall. Then the Bank of Manhattan Building, crumbling, partly falling sidewise, partly slumping upon the ruins of itself. Simultaneously the Chrysler Building toppled. For a second or two it seemed perilously to sway. Breathless, awesome seconds. It swayed over, lurched back like a great tree in a wind. Then very slowly it swayed again and did not come back. Falling to the east, its whole giant length came down in a great arc. The descent grew faster, until, in one great swoop it crashed upon the wreckage of the Grand Central Station. The roar of it surged over the city. The crash of masonry; the clatter of its myriad windows, the din of its rending, breaking girders.

The giant buildings were everywhere tumbling like falling giants; like Titans stricken by invisible tumors implanted in their vitals. It lasted ten minutes. What infinitude of horror came to proud and lordly Manhattan Island in those momentous ten minutes!

Ten thousand patrolling soldiers and police, bands of lurking criminals, and men, women and children who still had not left the city, went down to death in those ten minutes. Yet no observer could have seen them. Their little bodies, so small amid these Titans of their own creation, went into oblivion unnoticed in the chaos.

THE little solidifying bombs of the White Invaders did their work silently. But what a roar surged up into the moonlit night from the stricken city! What tumult of mingled sounds! What a myriad of splintering, reverberating crashes, bursting upward into the night; echoing away, renewed again and again so that it all was a vast pulsing throb of terrible sound. And under it, inaudible, what faint little sounds must have been the agonized screams of the humans who were entombed!

Then the pulse of the great roaring sound began slowing. Soon it became a dying roar. A last building was toppling here and there. The silence of death was spreading over the mangled litter of the strewn city. Dying chaos of sound; but now it was a chaos of color. Up-rolling clouds of plaster dust; and then darker, heavier clouds of smoke. Lurid yellow spots showed through the smoke clouds where everywhere fires were breaking up.

And under it, within it all, the vague white shapes of the enemy apparitions stood untouched, still peering curious, awed triumphant at what they had done.

Another ten minutes passed; then half an hour, perhaps. The apparitions were moving now. The many little groups were gathering into fewer, larger groups. One marched high in the air, with faint lurid green beams slanting down at the ruins of the city; not as weapons this time, but as beams of faint light, seemingly to illuminate the scene, or perhaps as signals to the ghostly army.

The warships in the Hudson were steaming slowly toward the Battery to escape. Searchlights from them, from the other ships hovering impotent in the bay, and from a group of encircling planes, flashed their white beams over the night to mingle with the glare of the fires and the black pall of smoke which was spreading now like a shroud.

THERE were two young men in a monoplane which had helplessly circled over mid-Manhattan. They saw the city fall, and noticed the lurking wraiths untouched amid the ruins and in the air overhead. And they saw, when it was over, that one great building very strangely had escaped. The Empire State, rearing its tower high into the serene moonlight above the wreckage and the rising layers of smoke, stood unscathed in the very heart of Manhattan. The lone survivor, standing there with the moonlight shining upon its top, and the smoke gathering black around its spreading base.

The two observers in the airplane, stricken with horror at what they had seen, flew mechanically back and forth. Once they passed within a few hundred feet of the standing giant. They saw its two hundred foot mooring mast for dirigibles rising above the eighty-five stories of the main structure. They saw the little observatory room up there in the mooring mast top, with its circular observation platform, a balcony around it. But they did not notice the figures on that balcony.

Then, from the top of the Empire State Building—from the circular observation platform—a single, horribly intense green light-beam slanted out into the night! A new attack! As though all which had gone before were not enough destruction, now came a new assault. The spectral enemies were tangible now!

THE single green light-beam was very narrow. But the moonlight could not fade it; over miles of distance it held visible. It struck first a passing airplane. The two observers in the monoplane were at this time down near the Battery. They saw the giant beam hit the airplane. A moment it clung, and parts of the plane faded. The plane wavered, and then, like a plummet, fell.

The beam swung. It struck a warship lying in the upper bay. Explosions sounded. Puffs of light flared. The ship, with all its passengers vanished and gone, lay gutted and empty.

The source of the light moved rapidly around the circular balcony. The light darted to every distant point of the compass. The surprised distant ships and forts, realizing that here for the first time was a tangible assailant, screamed shots into the night. But the green beam struck the ships and forts and instantly silenced them.

Now the realization of this tangible enemy spread very far. Within a few minutes, planes and radio communication had carried the news. From distant points which the light could not or did not reach, long-range guns were firing at the Empire State. A moment or two only. The base of the building was struck.

Then, frantically, observing planes sent out the warning to stop firing. The green beam had for a minute or two vanished. But now it flashed on again. What was this? The spectral wraiths of ten thousand of the enemy were staring. The observers in the planes stared and gasped. What fantasy! What new weird sight was this, stranger than all that had preceded it!

CHAPTER TWELVE
On the Tower Balcony

UPON the little observatory balcony at the top of the Empire State some twelve hundred feet above the stricken city, Don and I were with Tako as he erected the giant projector. In the midst of the silent shadowy outline of the stricken city falling around us, we had carried the projector up the mountain slope. The spectre of the Empire State Building was presently around us; we were in a hallway of one of the upper stories. Slowly, we materialized with our burden. I recall, as the dark empty corridor of the office building came to solidity around me, with what surprise I heard for the first time the muffled reverberations from the crumbling city....

We climbed the dark and empty stairs, upward into the mooring mast. Don and I toiled with the box, under the weapons of our two guards.

It was only a few minutes while Tako assembled and mounted the weapon. It stood a trifle higher than the parapet top. It rolled freely upon a little carriage mounted with wheels. Don and I peered at it. We hovered close to Tako with only one thought in our minds, Jane's murmured words—if we could learn something about this projector....

THEN the horror dulled us. We obeyed orders mechanically, as though all of it were a terrible dream, with only a vague undercurrent of reiterated thought: some chance must come—some fated little chance coming our way.

I recall, during those last terrible minutes when Tako flung the projector beam to send all his distant enemies hurtling into annihilation, that I stood in a daze by the parapet. Don had ceased to look. Tako was rolling the projector from one point to another around the circular balcony. Sometimes he was out of sight on the other side, with the observatory room in the mast hiding him.

We had been ordered not to move. The two guards stood with hand weapons turned on so that the faint green beams slanted downward by their feet, instantly ready, either for Don or me.

And I clung to the balcony rail, staring down at the broken city. It lay strewn and flattened as though, not ten minutes, but ten thousand years of time had crumbled it into ruins.

Then shots from the distant warships began screaming at us. With a grim smile, Tako silenced them. There was a momentary lull.

And then came our chance! Fate, bringing just one unforeseen little thing to link the chain, to turn the undercurrent of existing circumstances—and to give us our chance. Or perhaps Jane, guided by fate, created the opportunity. She does not know. She too was dazed, numb—but there was within her also the memory of what Tolla had almost said. And Tolla's frenzy of jealousy....

TAKO appeared from around the balcony, rolling the projector. Its beam was off. He flung a glance of warning at the two guards to watch us. He left the projector, flushed, triumphant, all his senses perhaps reeling with the realization of what he had done. He saw the two girls huddled in the moonlight of the balcony floor. He stooped and pushed Tolla roughly away.

"Jane! Jane, did you see it? My triumph! Tako, master of everything! Even of you—is it not so?"

Did some instinct impel her not to repulse him? Some intuition giving her strength to flash him a single alluring moonlit glance?

But suddenly he had enwrapped her in his arms. Kissing her, murmuring love and lust....

This was our chance. But we did not know it then. A very chaos of diverse action so suddenly was precipitated upon this balcony!

Don and I cried out and heedlessly leaped forward. The tiny beams of the guards swung up. But they did not reach us, for the guards themselves were stricken into horror. The shot from a far-distant warship screamed past. But that went almost unheeded. Tako had shouted, and the guards impulsively turned so that their beams missed Don and me.

Tolla had flung herself upon Tako and Jane. Screaming, she tore at them and all in an instant rose to her feet. Tako's cylinder, which she had snatched, was in her hand. She flashed it on as Don and I reached her.

THE guards for that instant could not fire for we were all intermingled. Don stumbled in his rush and fell upon Tako and Jane, and in a moment rose as the giant Tako lifted him and tried to cast him off.

My rush flung me against Tolla. She was babbling, mouthing frenzied laughs of hysteria. Her beam pointed downward, but as she reeled from the impact of my rush, the beam swung up; missed me, narrowly missed the swaying bodies of Tako and Don, and struck one of the guards who was standing, undecided what to do. It clung to him for a second or two, and then swung to the other guard.

The guards in a puff of spectral light were gone. Tolla stood wavering; then swung her light toward Tako and Don. But I was upon her.

"Tolla! Good God—"

"Get back from me! Back, I tell you."

I heard Jane's agonized warning from the floor. "Bob!"

Tolla's light missed my shoulder. Tako had cast Don off and stood alone as he turned toward us. Then Tolla's light-beam swung on him. I heard her eery maddened laugh as it struck him.

A wraith of Tako was there, stricken as though numbed by surprise.... Then nothingness....

Shots from the distant warships were screaming around us. One struck the base of the building.

I clung to my scattering senses. I gripped Tolla.

"That projector—what was it you almost told Jane?"

SHE stood stupidly babbling. "Told Jane? That projector—"

She laughed wildly, and like a tigress, cast me off. "Fools of men! Tako—the fool!"

She swung into a frenzy of her own language. And then back into English. "I will show you—Tako, the fool! All those fools out there under the ground and in the sky. I will show them!"

She stooped over the projector and fumbled with the mechanism.

Don gasped, "Those apparitions—is that what you're going to attack?"

"Yes—attack them!"

The beam flashed on. But it was a different beam now. Fainter, more tenuous; the hum from it was different.

It leaped into the ground. It was a spreading beam now. It bathed the white apparitions who were peering up at the city.

Why, what was this? Weird, fantastic sight! There was a moment of Tolla's frenzied madness; then she staggered away from the projector. But Don and I had caught the secret. We took her place. We carried it on.

We were hardly aware that the far-off warships had ceased firing. We hardly realized that Tolla had rushed for the parapet; climbed, screaming and laughing—and that Jane tried to stop her.

"Oh, Tolla, don't—"

But Tolla toppled and fell.... Her body was almost not recognized when it was later found down in the ruins.

Don and I flung this new beam into the night. We rolled the projector around the platform, hurling the beam in every direction at the white apparitions....

IT had caught first that group that lurked in the ground near the base of the Empire State. Tolla had turned the beam to the reverse co-ordinates from those Tako used. It penetrated into the borderland, reached the apparitions and forcibly materialized them! A second or two it clung to that group of white men's shapes in the ground. They grew solid; ponderable. But the space they now claimed was not empty! Solid rock was here, yielding space to nothing! Like the little materialization bombs, this was nature outraged. The ground and the solid rock heaved up, broken and torn, invisibly permeated and strewn with the infinitesimal atomic particles of what moments before had been the bodies of living men.

We caught with the beam that marching line of apparitions beneath the ground surface—a section of Tako's army that was engaged in a steady advance upon Westchester. The city streets over them surged upward. And some we caught under the rivers and within the waters of the bay, and the waters heaved and lashed into turmoil.

Then we turned the beam into the air. The apparitions lost contact with their invisible mountain peaks. And with sudden solidity, the gravity of our world pulled at them. They fell. Solid men's bodies, falling with the moonlight on them. Dark blobs turning end over end; plunging into the rivers and the harbor with little splashes of white to mark their fall; and yet others whirling down, crashing into the wreckage of masonry, into the pall of smoke and the lurid yellow flames of the burning city.

The attack of the White Invaders was over.

A YEAR has passed. There has been no further menace; perhaps there never will be. And again, the invisible realm of which Don, Jane and I were vouchsafed so strange a glimpse, lies across a void impenetrable. Earth scientists have the projector, with its current batteries apparently almost exhausted. And they have the transition mechanism which we three were wearing. But of those, the vital element had been removed by Tako—and was gone with him. Many others were found on the bodies, and upon the body of poor Tolla. But all were wrecked by their fall.

Perhaps it is just as well. Yet, often I ponder on that other realm. What strange customs and science and civilization I glimpsed.

Out of such thoughts one always looms upon me: a contemplation of the vastness of things to be known.

And the kindred thought: what a very small part of it we really understand!

THE END

Footnotes:

1. As we later learned, the scientific mechanism by which the transition was made from the realm of the fourth dimension to our own earthly world and back again, was only effective to transport organic substances. The green light-beam was of similar limitation. An organic substance of our world upon which it struck was changed in vibration rate and space-time co-ordinates to coincide with the characteristics with which the light-current was endowed. Thus the invaders used their beams as a weapon. The light flung whatever it touched of organic material with horrible speed of transition away into the Unknown—to the fourth, fifth, or perhaps still other realms. In effect—annihilation.

The mechanism of wires and dials (and small disks which were storage batteries of the strange current) was of slower, more controllable operation. Thus it could be used for transportation—for space-time traveling, as Earth scientists later came to call it. The invaders, wearing this mechanism, materialized at will into the state of matter existing in our world—and by a reversal of the co-ordinates of the current, dematerialized into the more tenuous state of their own realm.

2. We were soon to learn also that they were bringing into our world weapons, food, clothing and a variety of equipment by encasing the articles in containers operated by these same mechanisms of wires carrying the transition current. The

transportation was possible because all the articles they brought with them were of organic substance.

3.   The extent of the Fourth Dimensional world was never made wholly clear to us.   Its rugged surface was coincident with the surface of our earth at Bermuda, at New York City, and at many points along the Atlantic seaboard of the United States.   For the rest, there is no data upon which one may even guess.

4.   The vehicles were constructed of a material allied in character to that used for garments by the people of this realm.   It was not metal, but an organic vegetable substance.

5.   What we learned of the science of the invisible realm was perforce picked piecemeal by us from all that we saw, experienced, and what several different times Tako was willing to explain to us. And it was later studied by the scientists of our world, whose additional theories I can incorporate into my own knowledge.   Yet much of it remains obscure.   And it is so intricate a subject that even if I understood it fully I could do no more than summarize here its fundamental principles.

The space-transition of these vehicles, Tako had already told us, was closely allied to the transition from his world to ours.   And the weapons were of the same principles.   The science of space-transition, limited to travel from one portion of the realm to another, quite evidently came first.   The weapons, the forcible, abrupt transition of material objects out of the realm into other dimensions— into the Unknown—this principle was developed from the traveling.   And from them both Tako himself evolved the safe and controlled transition from his world to ours.

Concerning the operation of these vehicles: Motion, in our Earth-world or any other, is the progressive change of a material object in relation to its time and space. It is here now, but it *was there.* Both space and time undergo a simultaneous change; the object itself remains unaltered, save in its *position.*

In the case of the vehicles, the current I have already mentioned (used in the mechanism for the transition from Earth to the other realm) that current, circulating in the organic material of which the vehicle was composed, altered the state of matter of the carrier and everything within the aura of the current's field. The vehicle and all its contents, with altered inherent vibratory rate of its molecules, atoms and electrons, was in effect projected into another world. A new dimension was added to it. It became an imponderable wraith, resting dimly visible in a sort of borderland upon the fringe of its own world.

Yet it had not changed *position.* It still remained quiescent. Then the current was further altered, and the time and space co-ordinates set into new combinations. This change of the current was a *progressive* change. Controlled and carefully calculated by what intricate theoretic principles and practical mechanisms no scientist of our world can yet say.

It is clear, however, that as this progressive change in space-time characteristics began, the vehicle perforce must move slightly in space and time to reconcile itself to the change.

There never has been a seemingly more abstruse subject for the human mind to grasp than the theories involving a true conception of space-time. Yet, doubtless, to those of Tako's realm, inheriting, let me say, the consciousness of its reality, there was nothing abstruse about it.

An analogy may make it clearer. The vehicle, hovering in the borderland, might be called in a visible but gaseous state. A solid can be turned to gas merely by the alteration of the vibratory rate of its molecules.

This unmoving (gaseous) vehicle, is now further altered in space-time characteristics. Suppose we say it is very slightly thrown out of tune with its *spatial* surroundings at the time which is its *present*. Nature will allow no such disorganization. The vehicle, as a second of *time* passes, is impelled by the force of nature to be in a *different place*. This involves motion. A small change in the first second. Then the current alters it progressively faster. The change, of necessity, is progressively greater, the motion more rapid.

And this, controlled as to direction, became transportation. The determination of direction at first thought seems amazingly intricate. In effect, that was not so. With space-time factors set as a destination, i. e., the place where the vehicle must end its change at a certain time, all the intermediate changes become automatic. With every passing second it must be at a reconcilable place—the direction of its passage perforce being the shortest path between the two.

With this in mind, the transition from one world to another becomes more readily understandable. No *natural* change of space is involved, merely the change of the state of matter. It was the same change as that which carried the vehicles into a shadowy borderland, and then pushed further into new dimensional realms.

The green light-beam weapons were merely another application of the same principle. The characteristics of the green light current, touching organic matter, altered the vibratory rate of what was struck to coincide with the light. A solid cake of ice under a blow-torch becomes steam by the same principle. The light-beams were swift and violent in their action. The change in them was progressive also—but it was so swiftly violent a change that nothing living could survive the shock of the enforced transition.

6. Materialization bombs, we afterward called them; they played a diabolical part in the coming events. They were of many sizes and shapes, but most of them were small in size and shape, like a foot-long wedged-shaped brick, or the head of an ax. They were constructed of organic material, with a wire mesh of the transition mechanism encasing them, and an automatic operating device like the firing fuse of a bomb.

7. Neither Eunice Arton, nor any of the stolen girls, have ever been heard from since. Like the thousands of men, women and children who met

their death in the attack upon New York, Eunice Arton was a victim of these tragic events.

8.   The detailed nature of the scientific devices Tako used in the handling of his army during the attack never has been disclosed. I saw him using one of the eye-telescopes.   There was also a telephonic device and occasionally he would discharge a silent signal radiance—a curious intermittent green flare of light. His charts of the topography of New York City were to me incomprehensible   hieroglyphics—mathematical formula, no doubt; the co-ordinates of altitudes and contours of our world-space in its relation to the mountainous terrain of his world which stood mingled here with the New York City buildings.

9.   There was a thing which puzzled me before we arrived in the carrier, and surprised me when we left it; and though I did not, and still do not wholly understand it, I think I should mention it here. Traveling in the carrier we were suspended in a condition of matter which might be termed mid way between Tako's realm and our Earth-world. Both, in shadowy form, were visible to us; and to an observer on either world we also were visible.

Then, as the carrier landed, it receded from this sort of borderland as I have termed it, contacted with its own realm and landed. At once I saw that the shadowy outlines of New York were gone. And, to New York observers, the carriers as they landed, were invisible. The mountains—all this tumbled barren wilderness of Tako's world—were invisible to observers in New York.

But I knew now how very close were the two worlds—a very fraction of visible "distance," one from the other.

Then, with wires, disks and helmets—all the transition mechanism worn now by us and all of Tako's forces—we drew ourselves a very small fraction of the way toward the Earth-world state. Enough and no more than to bring it to most tenuous, most wraithlike visibility, so that we could see the shadows of it and know our location in relation to it, which was necessary to Tako's operations.

In this state, New York City was a wraith to us—and we were shadowy, dimly visible apparitions to New York observers. But in this slight transition, we did not wholly disconnect with the terrain of Tako's world. There was undoubtedly—if the term could be called scientific—a depth of field to the solidity of these mountains. By that I mean, their tangibility persisted for a certain distance toward other dimensions. Perhaps it was a greater "depth of field" than the solidity of our world possesses. As to that, I do not know.

But I do know, since I experienced it, that as we sat now encamped upon this ledge, the ground under us felt only a trifle different from when we had full contact with it. There was a lightness upon us—an abnormal feeling of weight-loss—a feeling of indefinable abnormality to the rocks. Yet, to observers in New York, we were faintly to be seen, and the rocks upon which we sat were not.